JUST A
LITTLE CHASE

NEW YORK TIMES BESTSELLING AUTHORS

Carly Phillips
Erika Wilde

She's in need of a fake, friendly boyfriend to charm her family.
He's the last bachelor up for auction and a grumpy, last-minute stand-in.
Neither satisfies the other's requirements but they might just be what each of them needs.

With Lauren Connelly's ex marrying her sister, the last thing she wants is to show up at the wedding without a date. Which means finding a fake boyfriend ASAP. The charity bachelor auction provides a solution to her problem, except the man she bids on turns out to be a gorgeous but grumpy executive who scowls more than he smiles.

Chase Gossard wants nothing to do with Lauren's plan to make him her plus-one at a destination wedding and pretend that he's in love. He doesn't do relationships, fake or otherwise—but she paid a lot of money for the privilege. So why does their touching, kissing, and sharing one bed feel all too real?

Lauren is smart and witty and sexy as hell. A down to earth combination that somehow softens his hard edges, and somewhere along the way, he's falling hard for his fake date. But when it's time to part ways, can the pretend girlfriend convince the confirmed bachelor to make things real?

Chapter One

LAUREN CONNELLY ATE a bite of her breakfast cereal, her gaze fixed on the wedding invitation she'd propped up against the saltshaker on the table. It wasn't every day that her little sister, Ashley, got married, and she should have felt excitement and joy for her sibling. Instead, she couldn't shake the dread at the thought of attending the nuptials and having to watch her sister marry the man Lauren had once been engaged to.

The entire situation was bound to be awkward and uncomfortable, made even more so by the small town mentality of where she'd been born and raised. It had always dumbfounded Lauren that there had been no scandalous gossip revolving around her sister's quick involvement with Greg after he'd broken up with Lauren. Rather, people looked at her with pity, because Greg had chosen the beauty pageant sister over the tomboy Lauren had been for most of her teenage years.

In Lauren's opinion, the town's perception was bullshit. Not many knew the real reason why their engagement had ended so abruptly, or that the two closest people to her at that time had deceived her. The truth would have blown up the gossip mill and branded Ashley as *the other woman*, and as much as her sister's actions had hurt Lauren, she'd never exposed their betrayal for a few different reasons. Lauren had never been the vindictive or spiteful type and she didn't want to fracture and divide their close family unit. And most importantly, long before she'd caught Ashley and Greg locked in a passionate kiss, she'd known that he wasn't "the one".

None of that excused the affair they'd had behind her back, but the painful breakup had been the impetus for Lauren to do the one thing she'd always dreamed of and leave her small Massachusetts town and move to New York City, where she now lived and worked as an event coordinator at the Meridian Hotel.

So, yes, awkward and uncomfortable was an understatement when Lauren thought about going back home for her sister's wedding.

"You know, if you stare at that invitation any harder, you're going to burn a hole in it," Lauren's roommate and good friend, Tara, commented, startling Lauren out of her pensive thoughts. "And that RSVP card is not going to send itself, by the way."

Lauren sighed as Tara settled into the chair across from her with a plate of avocado toast and a cup of coffee. "I know, I know," she said, setting her spoon in her cereal bowl. "I need to mail it this week. I've been dragging my feet because I want to take a plus-one to buffer things with my family, except I don't *have* a plus-one in my life." Because, unfortunately, the few men she'd met on dating apps had been complete duds. But maybe, possibly, she had an idea...

Tara grinned a bit mischievously and spoke before Lauren could share her thoughts. "You should shock the hell out of them and take a really bad boy to the wedding. Like a biker type. I could hook you up with someone from the shop, we could give *you* a few fake tattoos and body piercings—"

Lauren held up a hand to stop her friend's wild suggestion before it got even *more* outlandish, even though she was laughing at the image Tara painted. "Thank you for your offer, but no." A bad boy biker was more Tara's type. Her friend worked at a tattoo shop as a receptionist, had a full arm sleeve of colorful tattoos and a few extra piercings, and was drawn to rebellious men who bucked societal norms.

Tara feigned a pout, emphasizing the gold ring in her lip. "You're no fun."

Lauren grinned. "There's fun, and then there's giving my conservative parents a heart attack."

Tara rolled her eyes as she picked up her toast slathered in avocado. "Your straitlaced family could use a bit of shock and awe in their lives."

Lauren didn't disagree, but the last thing she wanted to do was draw unnecessary attention to herself while home for the wedding. She needed a low-key type of date, someone understated but attentive, so the gossip—and there was no doubt in her mind that there *would* be speculation about any man in her life—would lean toward Lauren having moved on from being dumped by her ex-fiancé for her sister, and was living a blissful life in NYC.

Lauren hated that she had to even consider such a ridiculous scenario in this day and age, but she couldn't change the small town mentality of where she'd grown up. Her parents constantly worried about her well-being despite Lauren assuring them she was doing well in the city. Then there was her eighty-three-year-old gramps whom she adored, and he worried about her, too. Throw in the town's old busybodies who felt sorry for her, and yeah, drastic measures were necessary.

All she wanted to do was blend in, not be the center of attention and gossip. With her ex having chosen her beauty queen sister, everyone would be watching Lauren's reactions, and if she had someone by her side, a man who deflected all that speculation, she wouldn't feel like the odd woman out.

Now that she'd vetoed Tara's suggestion to take a bad boy home, Lauren eyed the brochure sitting next to her cereal bowl, the one she'd grabbed from work on her way out the door on Friday. "So, about finding a plus-one to take to the wedding... I think I might have found a solution to that problem myself."

Interest sparkled in Tara's brown eyes. "Yeah, and what's that?"

"Remember me mentioning the upcoming Future Fast Track charity event I'm helping to organize at the Meridian?"

Tara nodded. "Yeah."

Biting her lower lip, and curious to hear what her friend thought about *her* unconventional idea, Lauren pushed the glossy booklet across the table to Tara. "They're having a bachelor auction at the event to raise money for the charity."

Her eyes went wide. "You're going to buy yourself a man?"

"I'm considering it." Lauren leaned back in her seat and shrugged. "Whatever man I win, he's committed to a weekend date, so it's the perfect arrangement. I wouldn't look dateless to my family or pathetic to the town gossips, and I'd be supporting a good cause. It's a win-win situation."

Tara flipped through the pages, quickly scanning the men up for auction and their profiles. "Meh," she said, a teasing smirk on her face. "They're all cleaned-up suits. Not a tattooed bad boy in the lot."

Lauren laughed. "Exactly. I don't want a man in a leather cut that grunts like a Neanderthal when spoken to," she said, about the type of biker guy Tara had described. "I want someone ordinary and friendly and educated, who can make small talk and pretend to be smitten with me. And when we get back home, we can go our separate ways, no muss, no fuss."

"Then yeah, buying yourself a man is the perfect solution," Tara said encouragingly as she pushed the closed brochure back to Lauren with a grin. "But if that doesn't work out for you, my offer to hook you up with a bad boy stands."

"Good to know." Decision made, Lauren reached for the RSVP card.

Grabbing a pen, she filled out the information and wrote in "2" for the number attending, then stuffed the card into its small envelope and sealed it closed so she could mail it on the way to work tomorrow morning.

One way or another, she was heading home for her sister's wedding with a charming, amiable date on her arm. Now, she just had to figure out which man to bid on at the auction.

CHASE GOSSARD CLOSED out his emails and for the fourth time, glanced at the clock on his phone, his annoyance growing. His half-sister, Billie, was late for their monthly lunch date, and because he'd arrived early at the café, he'd been sitting at the table waiting for the past half hour.

The waitress, a pretty young blonde, came by to refill his half-empty glass of iced tea. "Are you sure you don't want to go ahead and order?" she asked as she eyed him with appreciation, her gaze obviously taking in his tailored suit and the Hermès watch on his wrist before landing on his face. One he'd been told he could have graced fashion magazines with, not that he gave a shit.

"No," he replied, doing his best to tamp down his impatience. "She'll be here."

The waitress smiled playfully. "I sure hope so, be-cause any woman who would stand you up is a fool."

He refrained from rolling his eyes and gave her a tight smile instead. Clearly, she was fishing to see if he was single, and he didn't clarify that he was waiting on his sister, not an actual date.

She moved on to the next table, and he exhaled a deep breath. He wasn't interested in striking up a flirtatious conversation, which wasn't his forte, any-way. Having just gotten out of a *situationship* gone bad, he wasn't looking to jump into another. He didn't do committed relationships, which had been the issue with the last woman he'd been randomly hooking up with, only to discover *she* believed she'd be the one to change him.

Yeah, that hadn't ended well—it never did—and he'd put his dick's needs on hiatus. For now.

Chase picked up his phone again. He was just about to send Billie a "Where are you?" text, when she rushed out onto the restaurant patio and toward his table.

"Get that disapproving frown off of your face," she said with an infectious grin. His sister was one of the few people who was unaffected by his typical grumpy demeanor. "I'm fifteen minutes late because I got an important work call and I couldn't leave until I handled things. And I didn't have the chance to text *you* because I was finishing up that same call while riding in the Uber to get here. It took a huge amount of brainstorming to resolve a crisis involving this weekend's Future Fast Track charity event. It was business. You know how that is."

He immediately softened, his irritation melting away because he did understand that work was sometimes unpredictable and demanding, and mostly because Billie was his half-sister and he had a soft spot for her. She was one of the few people who could put a pin in his bluster and make him calm the fuck down.

Crazy, considering he'd only recently found out that she existed, and she'd only been in his life for a few years. He was a man who didn't let people in. Didn't let them get close or scale the emotional walls he'd erected as a young kid after his mother walked out on him and his father and never looked back. Yet this vivacious, free-spirited girl had knocked past his defenses and made a place for herself in his life as if she'd always belonged there.

She settled in across from him, out of breath from rushing. Her pretty face was flushed, and her unconventional pink highlighted hair was a bit tousled. But once she was settled in her seat, she flashed him one of those gregarious smiles of hers, the one that lit up her light blue eyes behind the black framed glasses she wore.

For a girl who'd been handed off to numerous foster homes growing up, her constant bright, upbeat attitude always amazed him.

They looked over the menu, and he didn't miss the disappointment in the server's eyes when she saw Billie there. There was a bit of confusion, too, because given his expensive suit, she'd probably been expecting a sophisticated woman to show up, instead of a young, quirky twenty-three-year-old with an eclectic fashion style that was as funky as her colored hair.

They placed their orders, and once the waitress delivered Billie's soda and they were alone again, he addressed the reason why she'd been so late.

"What's the big crisis at work?" he asked, always curious to hear about her job, which she loved. Future Fast Track, a nonprofit that was dedicated to helping foster kids as they aged out of the system, was near and dear to her heart, for good reason.

"The charity event is in two days, and one of the men in the bachelor auction came down with the latest flu virus and had to pull out," she said, unwrapping her straw and sticking it into her drink. "Finding a replacement in such a short time is more difficult than we'd expected and we *have* to fill his slot."

The fact that she was currently giving him those desperate, puppy dog eyes did not bode well for Chase, and a sense of dread filled his chest. She hadn't actually asked him to step in for the sick bachelor, but he knew, without a doubt, that's where this conversation was heading.

"There has to be some guy out there willing to step in," he said, quickly trying to deflect by offering some helpful advice. "A friend of a friend who's already part of the bachelor auction, or something."

She shook her head woefully. "My boss and I have been on the phone all morning, and no luck. It's totally stressing Aurora out, which is not good for a woman who is seven months pregnant." Billie loved the woman she worked for, who'd also grown up in the foster care system and understood the challenges kids experienced there.

Chase frowned at his sister. Was she really using the sympathy card? Yes, yes she was, the minx. "Do *not* look at me like that," he said, his voice a low, surly growl that didn't faze her in the least.

"Like what?" Behind her glasses, she batted her lashes much too guilelessly.

She knew exactly what she was doing, and he refused to offer up his services for something so appalling as a bachelor auction. "I have no desire to be paraded around like a show pony."

She laughed, the sound light and amused. "Give yourself some credit, Chase. You're definitely a stallion, not a show pony. You have the looks, you're an eligible bachelor, and as a corporate financier, you're a great catch. Any woman who reads your impressive bio and sees your photo will be willing to shell out big bucks to spend a weekend with you."

A fucking *weekend* entertaining a woman? He shuddered at the thought. Hell, he could barely tolerate a date for a few hours before he felt smothered and annoyed by her presence. "I'm not interested, Billie." His tone was firm.

"Interested, no…" Her voice trailed off for a few seconds as she bit her bottom lip. "But what about doing it for the sake of charity?"

He barely caught his scowl before it formed. "I've already donated a substantial amount to Future Fast Track over the past few years." And he'd done so willingly, and lovingly, because he understood how important the nonprofit was to her.

"I know, and you know I'm always grateful. But it's not the same thing because it's very behind the scenes and impersonal when you just hand over a check," she stressed, not relenting one iota. "No one but the charity knows that you're endorsing Future Fast Track. Being a part of the auction would show your support in a more visible way."

At that moment, their lunch arrived and he breathed a sigh of relief, hoping that if he didn't say anything more on the topic, the issue would magically disappear. He started on his turkey club, and she ate a few bites of her quiche. When she remained silent, the tension tightening his shoulders eased and he began to relax and enjoy his meal, certain he'd made his point.

No such luck.

"So, can I take your quiet internalizing as a yes?" she persisted.

He nearly choked on a bite of his sandwich. "*No*," he said once he swallowed, his voice emphatic and gruff. "And I'm not *internalizing* anything. I'm quiet because I'm trying to eat, for God's sake."

"Please?" Undeterred, she set her fork down and folded her hands together beneath her chin, her eyes imploring him. "Having you on that stage would mean the world to me, Chase."

It was those words that made his heart constrict in his chest, because they were honest and true and without any manipulating intent. The truth was, Billie never asked him for anything, when he wanted to give her everything she'd missed out on growing up because of their mother's shitty decisions—mainly, her choice to stay involved with Billie's deadbeat father who'd cared more about finding his next fix instead of his daughter's welfare.

When their mother died in a tragic car accident when Billie was eight—something Chase hadn't known until he'd hired a PI to find the sibling his own father had told him about on his death bed—he'd discovered that Billie's dad had surrendered her to child protective services shortly after Darlene's death. Because *he* didn't want to raise a child he'd never wanted in the first place. *Asshole.*

Chase had also learned from the investigative report that from the age of eight to when she'd aged out at eighteen, she'd been shuffled through a series of foster homes. Some decent, and others more problematic, the latter of which he didn't want to think about her enduring, all alone and afraid.

But despite her crappy childhood and the adversities she'd faced, she'd become a resilient young woman and a champion for other foster kids who needed help and guidance once they no longer had the support of the system. He was so damn proud of how well rounded and independent she was, how positively she viewed the world, despite her traumatic upbringing, when his own childhood had fucked with his head and left him skeptical and jaded.

Jesus, in some ways she had her shit together better than he did. At least emotionally and mentally.

As she continued to look at him with that hopeful expression on her face, a familiar guilt wove its way through him. He hadn't lived a charmed childhood. His father was rarely present and suffered from depression, requiring constant care, but Chase definitely had more stability and security than Billie ever experienced. He'd tried his best to make up for all of that now by spoiling her but his sister was such a simple creature when it came to what she needed and wanted from their relationship, and she'd told him many times she didn't want the things his money could buy. She only wanted an emotional and familial connection between them. Which was why he loved her so much.

She was so selfless when it came to others, and in the scheme of things, he was being a selfish dick by denying her the one thing she'd ever asked him for. Unfortunately for him, what she desired wasn't something his money could buy. It required him to step up and *show* Billie how much he supported the nonprofit she was so passionate about.

"Fine," he grumbled, still not thrilled at the prospect of being auctioned off to some random woman for a weekend. "I'll do it."

Billie beamed at him, her smile as bright as the early October sunshine warming the café patio. "Thank you, Chase. I knew you'd come through for me."

He narrowed his gaze, but softened his scowl with a hint of a smile, just for her. "Only because you were clearly determined to wear me down until I said yes."

"Maybe," she admitted impishly as she went back to her lunch, looking extremely pleased with herself. "Just a little."

He shook his head and resumed eating his sandwich, trying to resign himself to his fate.

Was he happy about the situation? Absolutely not. But for Billie, he'd suck up his discomfort and be the big brother she needed him to be.

Chapter Two

T HE DAY OF the Future Fast Track charity gala was chaos, but it was the kind of exhilarating hustle and bustle that Lauren loved about her job as an event coordinator for the Meridian Hotel. And with her boss, Jade Dare, on maternity leave, she was in charge and busier than usual.

From early morning to mid-afternoon that Saturday, she was caught up in a whirlwind of activity, from overseeing the setup and décor of the lavish ballroom for the formal dinner and fundraiser, to coordinating with Billie and Aurora at Future Fast Track to ensure that everything they'd requested was in place, to making sure the chef in charge of the catering crew had everything they needed for the five-course meal that would be served to the guests.

Once Lauren felt confident that everything was ready for the evening's festivities, she'd rushed home to change into something more appropriate for a formal gala. She'd chosen a comfortable burgundy gown with a skirt that was more billowy than formfitting so she could move around quickly and easily, just in case there were any potential issues that might arise that she needed to take care of during the course of the event.

While Aurora and Billie encouraged her to enjoy the festivities, Lauren was always aware that she was still on the job and had her eyes on everything as the evening progressed, making sure the event ran smoothly and efficiently. There were small fires to put out, which was normal for any big venue, but for the most part the welcome reception and dinner went off without a hitch, much to her relief.

By the time the bachelor auction was announced, Lauren found herself relaxing a bit, since the most crucial parts of the evening were now behind her. She met up with her coworker and good friend, Skye, and accompanied her as they joined the rest of the single women gathering around the stage.

"So, I told Tripp yes to his offer," Skye said once they'd found a place, referring to her old flame she'd recently hooked up with and the fact that he'd volunteered to give Skye the baby she wanted so badly—by impregnating her the old-fashioned way instead of the insemination process she'd originally planned on. "And he asked me to bid on him, no matter the amount, so that he wouldn't have to spend the weekend with any other woman."

Grinning, Lauren looped her arm through Skye's, happy for her friend, and equally impressed that Tripp—as one of the bachelors up for auction—had his sights set on only one particular female in the crowd. "That's because he's a stand-up guy with morals and integrity. I mean, why would he want another woman when he has you?"

A blush swept across Skye's cheeks as she rolled her eyes at Lauren. "He doesn't *have* me."

Lauren waggled her brows playfully. "Well, technically he will be 'having you' for the foreseeable future until you get pregnant."

Skye shook her head at Lauren's comment, but was smiling as they watched all the bachelors gradually take their places on the stage. Lauren didn't miss the way her friend's eyes remained on Tripp, who'd also found her in the throng of women and gave her a sexy smile that made Skye blush all over again.

As the men continued to take their positions, Skye managed to tear her gaze from Tripp to glance at Lauren. "Okay, so which guy did you decide on for yourself?" she asked curiously.

Considering they worked together, and were good friends, Lauren had told Skye about her idea of buying a bachelor to take to her sister's wedding when they'd gone out for drinks the previous weekend. After solidifying her plan with Tara, Lauren had taken a good, long look at her options and had settled on a guy she deemed the best man for the job as her fake boyfriend.

"His name is Neil Pierson, and according to the information he sent in, he's an accountant," she told Skye, waiting for the man to arrive onstage so she could get an in-person glimpse of him. She hoped he at least looked somewhat like his photo, which had depicted a mild-mannered, but decent-looking guy. "I decided to go for someone boring but dependable who will hopefully be willing to fake date me at my sister's wedding and help convince my family I really *am* happy."

"Which one is he?" Skye asked curiously.

Lauren frowned, realizing that all the other men in the brochure had taken their places, except for Neil. "In the brochure, he was the last guy listed, but his spot is empty."

Skye patted the arm that Lauren still had linked through hers in a reassuring manner. "I'm sure he's just making his way through the crowd to the stage."

Lauren nodded, because that probably was the case.

Her cellphone, which she'd tucked into the pocket of her gown, vibrated. Hoping it wasn't someone on the Meridian staff texting with a problem she needed to handle, she pulled out the device and was surprised to see a text from her mother instead. She opened it up and read the message.

I know you're at a work event this evening, but I wanted to let you know that Gramps had a mini stroke this afternoon. It was very mild and he's already home from the hospital and is doing fine, so there's no need to call tonight.

Despite her mother's reassuring words, panic surged through Lauren at the thought of anything happening to her gramps.

"Crap, I need to call home," Lauren said, her stomach twisting with anxiety as she glanced at Skye.

"Apparently, my grandfather had a mini stroke earlier this afternoon. My mom says it was mild and not overly serious, and he's already home from the hospital, but I need to hear for myself that he's okay."

"Of course," Skye said, giving her an understanding nod as the auctioneer started addressing the crowd around the stage. "Go and call."

"Hopefully I'll be back in time to bid on the last guy," Lauren said, then quickly headed out of the ballroom to find a quiet place to talk.

She decided on the women's lounge, which was empty—of course, since every female was back in the ballroom ogling the bachelors—and Lauren rang her mother's cell.

Her mom immediately picked up. "I told you that you didn't need to call," she said by way of greeting.

"Of course I'm going to call," Lauren replied, feeling her throat tighten with worry as she paced the length of the lounge. "How is Gramps? Should I head home? I could probably be there by midnight if I leave within the hour—" She could make the drive from New York City to just outside of Springfield, Massachusetts, in about two and a half hours.

"No," her mother said in an adamant tone. "There's no need for you to rush home."

Lauren exhaled a deep breath, knowing if there was a true medical emergency, her mother wouldn't hesitate to tell her to come. And since her gramps lived with her parents, she knew he was in good hands and well cared for.

"He's okay. I promise," her mother went on in a gentler tone. "He had what's known as a transient ischemic attack, which is like a mini stroke, but the effects are temporary. They did a CT scan at the hospital and there's no long-term damage, thank goodness, but they are taking precautions. They put him on dipyridamole. We're keeping an eye on his blood pressure, and he has an appointment to see his doctor on Monday. If you need any other reassurance that he's fine, then let me tell you he was as ornery as ever with the nurses."

That made Lauren smile.

"I don't like being stuck with needles like a human pin cushion!" her gramps grumbled from somewhere in the background.

"See, I told you." Her mother sighed, and Lauren could only imagine what a long day she'd had at the hospital. "I wasn't going to send you a message tonight because I know you're busy with your big charity event, but I also knew you'd be upset if you found out later."

"You're right. So thank you for letting me know." She sat down in one of the plush velvet chairs. "Can I talk to Gramps real quick?" She just wanted to hear for herself that he was okay.

"Of course."

Lauren heard the sound of the cellphone being transferred over to her gramps, then he spoke. "Hey, Scouty!" he said in that boisterous voice of his, proving there was nothing frail about this man who'd recently turned eighty-three.

Her heart lightened at the sound of the nickname he'd given her as a toddler, and still used. Scout/Scouty, because growing up she'd always been his little sidekick adventurer. She'd followed him around the small farm where her grandparents once lived, mucking out stalls, riding his tractor, and fishing with him on Sunday afternoons. All the things her frilly sister, Ashley, didn't want anything to do with.

"How's my girl?" he asked affectionately.

Her fingers tightened around her cellphone. "I'm good, Gramps. I can't wait to see you at the wedding next month." It had been too long since she'd been home and really spent time with the family.

"Me, too," he said, his voice a bit melancholy. "Your mother says you're bringing a beau to the wedding. I can't wait to meet this new man in your life and see if he's good enough for my girl."

Lauren wasn't surprised that her gramps knew about her plus-one, since her mother had received the RSVP card Lauren had sent earlier that week. She'd texted briefly with her mom after it arrived, and managed to avoid giving her any details about the guest she was bringing to the wedding. She'd wanted to see what happened tonight at the bachelor auction, before she shared a name or background information about the man she was "currently dating".

And speaking of which… Lauren heard the echo of the auctioneer banging his gavel against his podium and awarding some lucky woman a weekend with the bachelor she'd bid on, and apparently won. Lauren had no idea how many men were left standing, but she needed to get back into the ballroom before she lost the opportunity to grab Neil the accountant for her weekend home.

"Gramps, I'm so glad you're okay," she said, standing and smoothing a hand down the front of her gown. "I need to get back to the charity event, but I promise to call you tomorrow."

"Okay, Scouty," he said. "Love you, girl."

"Love you, too."

Lauren disconnected the call, and hoping she wasn't too late, she rushed back toward the ballroom. She passed the meet and greet area, seeing Skye there with Tripp, along with a lot of other couples who'd been paired off and were getting acquainted.

She arrived back in the ballroom just as the second to last man was auctioned off, leaving one bachelor left. Neil Pierson, she assumed, except as she moved closer to the stage and he stepped into the spotlight, she realized this man was *not* the staid accountant that had been advertised in the brochure.

No, he was the epitome of drop-dead gorgeous, and had quite the commanding presence in his fitted tuxedo. She couldn't help but admire his broad shoulders and the rest of his perfectly proportioned body—tall and lean and sexy as sin.

She lifted her gaze to his face, and a jolt of attraction shot through her as she catalogued his classically handsome features, taking in his prominent chin, his angular, clean-shaven jaw, and straight nose. His dark brown eyes matched the equally rich color of his hair, which was combed back and parted to the side.

For a man who exuded so much physical alphaness, he appeared extremely uncomfortable standing on the stage while the auctioneer introduced him to the masses as Chase Gossard, a replacement bachelor for Neil Pierson who'd gotten sick with the flu, then rattled off his attributes as a single, eligible bachelor who worked as a corporate financier.

That tight, less-than-affable smile on his face was like a deterrent in itself. Chase looked like he wanted to be anywhere but on the stage as the center of attention and up for grabs to the highest bidder. It didn't help matters that the downward slant of his eyebrows made him look intense and intimidating enough to scare off any potential dates.

Off to the side Lauren saw an exasperated Billie trying to get his attention, and when Chase glanced her way and she pointed to the exaggerated grin on her face—as if to encourage him to turn that frown upside down—he attempted to smile, which looked more like an unpleasant grimace.

Lauren would have laughed at the man's gloomy disposition, if he hadn't been her only choice available.

"Okay, ladies," the auctioneer said once his initial spiel was over. "He's the final man standing and your last chance at a weekend date with an eligible bachelor. Who'll start the opening bid?"

Shockingly, the room went quiet, and as Lauren

glanced around at the remaining women, she saw varying degrees of wariness and hesitancy to bid on him. Lauren had no idea how much the previous bachelors had sold for, but clearly Chase's standoffish demeanor wasn't doing him any favors. Unfortunately for her, if she wanted a date for her sister's wedding, he was her only option, and she was desperate enough to take a chance on him.

"Five thousand dollars!" she called out, her voice filling the silent ballroom.

She heard the surprised gasps, but what Lauren wasn't prepared for was the way Chase's gaze immediately sought her out, stunning her with the surprise that flickered in his eyes. Had he actually been secretly hoping that no one would bid on him? Or was he shocked that someone actually had, despite his less-than-charismatic personality?

His gaze locked on hers, and how was it that someone so seemingly aloof could jump-start her pulse and leave her a little breathless with those intense, dark eyes of his?

She caught the subtle arch of his brow, as if he were questioning her daring and reckless bravery when every other woman had interpreted his body language correctly, that he was no Prince Charming. His eyes asked her, almost mockingly, *Are you sure this is what you want?*

Considering she'd already blurted out an amount, it was too late to turn back now, so she straightened her shoulders and arched her own brow right back at him, just to show him that she wasn't at all intimidated by his big, bad wolf persona.

The corner of his mouth twitched with what she could only interpret as an amused smirk.

The auctioneer continued to encourage more bids, but no one else topped Lauren's amount. There was zero competition for Chase Gossard—surprise, surprise—and as the auctioneer banged his gavel and awarded her the man standing on the stage, Lauren felt a mixture of relief and annoyance. Relief, because he hadn't cost her a small fortune, and annoyance because this was *not* the man she'd had her sights set on.

The auctioneer instructed Lauren to meet up with Chase in the greeting area, just outside the ballroom. Wanting to get their initial introduction cemented before she needed to get back to work, she headed in that direction and ran into Skye just as she was returning from her own meet and greet with Tripp.

"Hey, how is your grandfather?" she asked, worry evident in her voice.

"He's okay," Lauren said, appreciating her friend's concern, and gave her a quick rundown of what her mother had told her. "He's at home resting and he'll have to see his doctor on Monday, but my mother assured me he's going to be fine, and I don't need to rush home when I'll be there for my sister's wedding next month."

"Good." Skye looked relieved on Lauren's behalf. "Did you make it back to the stage in time to bid on a bachelor?"

Lauren groaned, the sound filled with dread. "Yes, and I ended up with Mr. Grumpy Pants, not Neil Pierson the dependable accountant I was expecting. By the time I got back to the ballroom, he was the only one left and I just panicked and didn't let that scowl deter me from bidding on him. Not that I had much competition," she muttered.

Skye bit her bottom lip. "What happened to Neil? Did the auctioneer say?"

"Apparently he got sick with the flu, so this Chase guy was his last-minute replacement," she explained. "Billie must have been desperate to find someone, because he did not look happy to be up on that stage. But at least I got him dirt cheap."

"Well, that's a plus, at least," Skye said with a smile, trying to be positive.

Lauren sighed. "I'm on my way out to the greeting area to meet him. Keep your fingers crossed that I can persuade him to accompany me to my sister's wedding next month for our weekend together."

"You've got this." In a show of support, Skye held up both hands, fingers crossed for double the luck. "Go dazzle him with your beauty and charm, and I'll handle checking in with the Meridian service staff to make sure everything is still running smoothly."

Lauren straightened her shoulders and attempted her own smile. "He doesn't look like the type to be bowled over by beauty and charm, but I'll certainly try my best."

They parted ways, and Lauren walked out of the

ballroom and headed toward the meet and greet area, seeing Chase already there, standing off to the side. He had an impatient look on his gorgeous face—which unfortunately did nothing to lessen her attraction to him, *sigh*—and she wasn't surprised to see him push back the sleeve of his tuxedo jacket to check the watch strapped to his wrist, as if he were ticking down the minutes to when he could leave.

She refrained, just barely, from rolling her eyes.

Under any other circumstance she would have given this man a wide berth and avoided him completely. But she didn't have that luxury. He was hers for a weekend, bought and paid for, and she planned to at least get her money's worth.

WHEN CHASE AGREED to stand in as a replacement bachelor at the auction for Billie, he knew he'd hate the entire ordeal, and that had proven to be true. Standing onstage had been uncomfortable and awkward as fuck, and despite Billie trying to encourage him from the sidelines to smile and charm the women in the crowd, he hadn't been able to pretend to be anyone's fairytale hero. Faking *anything*, especially a particular emotion, wasn't in his genetic makeup.

What Chase hadn't counted on was a bold and beautiful brunette not giving a damn about his grimacing smile or unenthusiastic participation, and actually bidding on him. There had been a moment between them, right after she'd shouted out *five thousand dollars*, when he'd arched a brow at her, questioning her sanity and courage for even *wanting* a date with a man who was clearly less than thrilled to be a bachelor up for auction.

She didn't seem to care and had arched her brow right back at him. She'd been assertive and determined despite all the reasons why she should have steered clear of him, just as the other women had, and he'd been silently impressed with her gumption. And, admittedly, a bit turned on. He was used to women backing down in the face of his imposing personality, not challenging him, as this one had.

The fact that this woman's actions intrigued Chase made him all the more determined to get the hell out of there before he found himself spending the rest of the evening "getting to know her", which wasn't part of his plan. Yes, he'd fulfilled his obligation to Billie and stood in for the guy who'd been sick, and he intended to make it worth this woman's while for bidding on him for the sake of charity. But, he had absolutely no intentions of actually spending an entire weekend with her doing... well, anything.

Besides, she was probably already harboring regrets for bidding on him so spontaneously, like an impulsive purchase that seemed exciting at the time, until the reality of the situation set in. He was hardly the kind of charismatic guy the rest of the bachelors had been, and instead of the two of them spending a boring and awkward weekend together, he'd make sure she walked away from this transaction satisfied, nonetheless.

As he continued to wait in the meet and greet area for her to arrive, he shifted impatiently on his feet and checked the time on his watch, beyond ready to call it a night.

"Is there somewhere more important you need to be?" a cheeky female voice asked.

Chase lifted his head at the audacious question, watching the woman who'd won him approach where he was standing, her pink lips quirked in a very slight, but humorous smile.

That wasn't what he'd been expecting at all. Wariness or trepidation at meeting him, possibly. But a woman regarding him with amusement was quite the anomaly for him, and he wasn't sure what to do with that.

"Yes," he lied, thrown completely off-kilter by the pure, physical awareness that flooded his veins, especially when she was the complete opposite of the type of women he normally dated. She was understated and naturally pretty, in a fresh-faced, girl-next-door type of way.

While most of the other women at the gala wore sleek, sexy, head-turning gowns, the lower half of her burgundy-hued dress was loose instead of formfitting, skimming her curves instead of accentuating them. Her seemingly low maintenance hair was worn down in what appeared to be natural waves, and her makeup was so minimal that he could see the faint sprinkling of freckles over the bridge of her nose and along her cheeks.

Her full, soft-looking lips were distracting as hell, or maybe it was the way her eyes danced with more of that unexpected humor that completely unbalanced his equilibrium.

"You really have somewhere else you need to be?" she asked, tipping her head to the side and unabashed-ly challenging him again.

"I'm only here as a favor to my sister," he replied, his tone gruff.

That part was all truth, and he figured he'd be up-front and honest about his reasons for participating in the auction. He hadn't willingly volunteered but had been coerced into it.

She nodded as if understanding and pushed her hands into the pockets hidden in the voluminous skirt of her dress. "Ahh, so your arm was well and truly twisted. I'd be a bit crabby myself if a sibling pressured me into doing this, too," she replied, brazenly calling him out on his behavior and attitude.

He was so caught off guard by her sense of humor that a surprising chuckle almost escaped him. He managed, just barely, to maintain his staid composure.

"Who is your sister?" she asked curiously.

"Billie," he replied.

Her pretty brown eyes widened in shock. "Wait. Billie *Coale* is your sister?"

He heard the confusion in her voice, since he and Billie had different last names. "Yes. She's my half-sister."

"Oh, that explains *everything*," she said, as if he'd just clarified the wonders of the universe.

Chase frowned. He was an intelligent man, but he had no clue what she meant or what she was referring to. "What does that explain, exactly?"

"The vast differences in your personalities," she said, and dared to grin. "You're half-siblings, so clearly Billie got all the bright, warm, positive qualities in her half of your shared DNA, and you were left with the cantankerous, grumpy traits."

Her tongue-in-cheek analysis of their significantly contrasting personalities would have amused Chase if she hadn't nailed it all so accurately. This woman had no idea how much truth her seemingly innocuous statement held.

"I'm Lauren Connelly, by the way," she said, introducing herself and changing the course of their conversation.

She removed her right hand from her pocket and extended it toward him. He slid his hand into hers, trying to ignore her warm, soft skin and how slender her fingers felt clasped in his larger, stronger ones. He held on longer than he should have, and couldn't even explain why except that he liked touching her. Even crazier, he also enjoyed seeing the flash of awareness in her eyes as he skimmed his thumb along the back of her hand.

"It's nice to meet you," he said, and shockingly, he meant it.

She gave him a teasing grin as she pulled her arm back, forcing him to release her hand. "Aww, you don't need to start being polite now."

He huffed out a laugh, the sound rough from disuse. God, this one had moxie, and she was so transparent and real. He'd been expecting a rich, spoiled socialite to win him, not this unpretentious, feisty, down-to-earth woman who had no qualms about calling him out. As he felt something shift inside of him and his guard lower a few inches, he quickly reminded himself that he had no intention of spending any significant amount of time with her.

He cleared his throat and ran a hand along his jaw, forcing himself to treat this as a business transaction and do what needed to be done. "I'm sure you didn't mean to bid on me, though you did do me a favor by doing so and I'm happy to repay you very generously."

Her gaze narrowed on him. "What do you mean?"

He exhaled a deep breath and shoved his own hands into the front pockets of his slacks. "I mean, I'm happy to write you a check to reimburse you for the amount you bid on me, plus a substantial bonus for pain and suffering—"

She laughed, as he'd secretly hoped she would at that last part of his statement. "Pain and suffering are apt descriptions considering your pessimist attitude."

He tried again, this time opting for a bit of honesty. "Look, I'm the last man you want to spend a weekend with."

"I'm sure you're right about that," she agreed,

though her eyes still sparkled amicably. "But you're not getting off that easy. I need a man for a particular weekend, and for a specific reason, and you're going to have to do."

Before she could elaborate—because he was curious as hell to know those details, even though they wouldn't change his mind—he heard a slight buzzing sound. She pulled her cellphone from her pocket and frowned as she read whatever text message had come through.

She cursed beneath her breath, then lifted her gaze back to his. "I need to go. I'm the event coordinator here at the Meridian and I'm technically still on the clock. The bartender just broke a glass and cut his hand and I need to address the issue."

He nodded in understanding and quickly withdrew a business card from the pocket inside his tuxedo jacket. "Here. Take this. Give my secretary a call next week and we'll come up with a mutually satisfactory way to resolve this situation."

A frown furrowed her brow at his choice of words as she took his business card. "Actually, here's *my* information," she said, quickly turning the tables on him as she pulled her own business card from the credit card holder attached to the back of her phone case and handed it to him. "Why don't *you* give me a call and we'll discuss the particulars of our weekend together?"

She was adorably persistent and determined, but yeah, hanging out with her for a weekend, for any reason, wasn't going to happen.

Another message buzzed through on her phone, grabbing her attention once again. "I really do need to go. Have a nice rest of your evening, Chase."

He gave her a curt nod. "You, too, Lauren."

He watched her head back into the ballroom, surprised by the stab of regret he felt as she walked away.

Clearly, it was time for him to go, because he had a feeling if he stayed he'd spend that time watching her, and contemplating what he might be possibly letting go, and giving up, with a woman like her.

Ending things now was for the best. She was much too nice and sweet, even beneath that feisty exterior, and he was… well, he wasn't anything she needed in her life.

Chapter Three

L AUREN WONDERED HOW long it would take Chase to contact her. After their interesting interaction and conversation at the charity event, they'd left things at an impasse. He'd told her to call his assistant, and she'd told Chase to call *her*.

And what the hell did he mean by *we'll come up with a mutually satisfactory way to resolve this situation*, anyway? In her mind, there was only one way to settle things, and that was by him stepping up to be her fake boyfriend for a weekend trip home for her sister's wedding. There was no other reason for her to have bid on him.

She got the distinct impression that Chase was a man used to making demands and getting his way, and because of that she didn't expect a call on Monday. She wasn't even surprised when Tuesday went by without a word, either, which meant he was most likely waiting for *Lauren* to pick up the phone and ring his assistant so he wouldn't have to talk to her.

It was now Wednesday afternoon, and as Lauren sat in her office at the Meridian and reviewed a vendor list for an upcoming wedding, she estimated she had a few more days that she could wait Chase out. She had every intention of forcing him to step up and follow through on the obligation he obviously had no desire to fulfill as a purchased bachelor—even though, for some reason, he'd agreed to step into Neil Pierson's vacant spot, all for his half-sister, Billie.

From the little she'd gleaned about Chase in the short time she'd been in his presence, she'd learned the man was a paradox. Indulgent when it came to Billie, but a formidable, assertive opponent in other aspects of his life, like business. He clearly wasn't used to anyone bucking his authority, but Lauren was equally strong-willed, and she refused to let Chase dictate how this "arrangement" would go.

The grumpy, cantankerous Chase Gossard was not Lauren's first choice of a date. Not by a long shot, but since she'd been given a sourpuss lemon, she was going to do her damnedest to make sweetened lemonade out of Chase, and their situation. She'd always been a "look on the bright side of things" kind of girl, and this predicament was no different.

In fact, she was so confident that Chase would be accompanying her to her sister's wedding, that when she spoke to her mother and Gramps on Monday to check in, she'd actually dropped his name to them. And after googling him and discovering he was a successful and wealthy corporate financial advisor, and partner at a prestigious investment firm in Manhattan, she'd mentioned that to them, as well, impressing the hell out of her family that she'd landed such a catch.

So, yeah, there was no way she was going to let Chase back out and leave her hanging out to dry, facing yet another humiliating rejection from a man, as far as her family would be concerned.

The ringing of her cellphone startled Lauren out of her thoughts. She glanced at the display, expecting a business call, and was surprised to see the name "Chase" on the display, which she'd typed into her cell, along with his office number.

Feeling a bit victorious that he'd broken first, she put the call on speaker and answered with a cheerful, chipper, "Hello."

"Hi, is this Lauren?"

She frowned at the unfamiliar female voice on the line, just as Skye walked into her office. Lauren lifted a finger to let her friend know to wait a second while she replied to the caller on the phone. "Yes, this is her."

"Oh, good!" the woman said in a friendly, enthusiastic tone. "I'm calling for Chase Gossard. I'm his personal assistant, Victoria."

Irritation quickly replaced Lauren's momentary glee. Across her desk, even Skye's brows rose in surprise. "Could he not call me himself?" she asked, trying her best not to take her annoyance out on Victoria, who was just doing her job.

"Well, he really didn't see any need for that, since I've taken care of all the arrangements for the weekend you purchased," she said, clearly an assistant who was efficient in smoothing ruffled feathers.

Except Lauren was far from placated. "I'd like to speak to him directly about that, please."

"Oh, no need," Victoria insisted blithely. "I've booked a weekend for you and a person of your choice at Casa Cipriani in Lower Manhattan. You'll enjoy a stay in the Verrazzano two-bedroom suite, along with the butler's package, and a complete spa day. Fine dining is included for both nights, along with a Broadway show, and a twenty-thousand-dollar shopping spree at Oscar de la Renta on Madison Avenue."

Holy shit. Lauren's head spun as she listened to Victoria's spiel, while Skye's eyes widened and her jaw dropped open in shock at what the other woman was offering… a weekend of a lifetime that most women would be thrilled to have.

Being in the hospitality business, Lauren knew that Casa Cipriani was an exclusive members' club and hotel, and their suites were an obscene amount of money per night, *without* butler service. Add in a spa day, fine dining, a Broadway show, and a twenty-thousand-dollar shopping spree, and the cost for the weekend was almost beyond Lauren's comprehension.

Then again, for a wealthy businessman like Chase, it was nothing more than a piddly little write-off. A drop in the bucket. And if she accepted, he could wipe his conscience clean and consider his bachelor auction duties done and over with.

She wasn't about to let him off so easily.

"I just need to know what dates work best for you

and I'll handle everything else," Victoria said, when she was finally finished trying to wow Lauren with her long-winded sales pitch.

Very calmly, despite the urge to scream, Lauren asked once again, "Can I talk to Chase, please?"

"I'm very sorry, but he's not available."

Lauren ground her teeth and called bullshit. "Is he in the office?"

"Yes, but—"

"For the afternoon?" Lauren stood and retrieved her purse from the bottom drawer of her desk.

"Yes, but—"

Perfect. "I'll be by to speak to him within the next hour."

"I don't think—"

Lauren disconnected the call, not caring at all what Victoria thought. This issue was between her and Chase, and clearly required a face-to-face conversation. If he thought he could buy her off, he was sadly mistaken. Out of pure principal alone, she was going to make him follow through on his end of the deal.

"Are you really going to his office?" Skye asked as Lauren pulled out the business card Chase had given her, which had his building's address.

"Yep." She opened the Uber app on her phone and ordered a ride, just as her cell rang again with Chase's name on the display. She sent the call straight to voice mail, not in the mood to deal with platitudes over the phone.

Skye bit her lower lip as Lauren swept past her and

out of her office. "Should I be worried?" her friend asked from behind her.

Lauren laughed, even though there was nothing funny about what was about to go down between her and Mr. Grumpy Pants. "No, but Chase Gossard should be."

Because Lauren Connelly wasn't anyone's pushover, and she wasn't about to start now.

✧　✧　✧

CHASE WAS IN the conference room reviewing a client's investment portfolio with one of the firm's junior financial advisors, when he heard raised voices coming from his personal assistant's desk. Frowning, he paused mid-sentence, and the silence between himself and Gary gave him the chance to overhear the conversation happening just down the hall.

"I'm really sorry that you made a trip here," Victoria said, sounding flustered, when she was normally so composed. "But I already told you on the phone that Mr. Gossard is not available. He's in a meeting for the afternoon and asked not to be interrupted."

That was true. While reviewing the portfolio with Gary, and discussing stock options and other investments for their multibillionaire client, Chase had told Victoria to put all his calls on hold for the afternoon. The last thing he'd wanted was constant distractions diverting his attention.

"That's fine," a familiar female voice replied, and

there was no mistaking the determination in her tone. "I have nowhere else I need to be for the rest of the afternoon, so I'll just sit right here in this reception area and wait until he is available, because I'm not leaving until I've spoken to him personally."

Yep, there was only one woman in his recent memory who'd shown such tenacity when it came to dealing with him. Lauren Connelly. Except he had no idea why she'd shown up at his office, when he'd instructed Victoria to call Lauren with what he felt was a very generous offer, in lieu of any weekend with him.

A minute later, his personal assistant walked into the conference room, her face flushed. "I know you said not to bother you, but Lauren Connelly is here," she said, keeping her voice low.

"I heard," he said wryly. "*Why* is she here? Didn't you get in touch with her earlier about compensating her for the bachelor auction?"

She nodded, wringing her hands together. "Yes, but she wasn't very happy about the offer, and now she's insisting on speaking with you personally. She's adamant that she'll wait for however long that takes."

If it had been anyone else who'd been that forward and making demands, he would have been annoyed, but it didn't escape his notice that he was more curious, than irritated, when it came to Lauren.

He glanced at Gary, a young up-and-coming advisor in their firm, who had a few financial tabs open on his computer. "Let me handle this issue, and then we'll finish our discussion," Chase said, standing. "In the meantime, come up with some viable stock options for our client, and we'll analyze those opportunities when I get back."

"Will do," Gary replied, and began tapping away on the laptop's keyboard.

Chase followed Victoria to the reception area, and as soon as Lauren saw him, she popped up from where she'd been sitting on one of the couches. Her chin lifted stubbornly, and her back straightened, as if she was squaring off to do battle. With him, apparently.

"I know you're a busy man, but I'm here to tell you that I'm not accepting your bribe."

Her word choice made him blink in surprise. "My bribe?"

"Isn't that what that big, fancy weekend package was all about?" she asked, bristling as she strode toward him, then stopped a few inches away. "A bribe so *you* wouldn't have to spend a weekend with me?"

She clearly wasn't happy with the arrangements he'd told Victoria to make, and whatever Lauren's reasons, he'd rather not have an audience while they discussed them. "Why don't we finish this conversation in my office, where it's more private?" he suggested.

"I think that's a good idea," she agreed with a decisive nod.

Trying to be a gentleman, he touched his hand to her lower back to guide her down the hall to his office. The silky fabric of her blouse was cool against his fingertips, which quickly gave way to the warmth of her skin beneath. He could have sworn he heard her suck in a breath as he increased the pressure of his palm and ushered her into the room. And that reaction gave him a great sense of satisfaction because he found he liked shaking up this woman's composure and throwing her off-kilter.

As soon as they were inside, she bolted away, severing the connection between them. But when she turned around to face him, her cheeks were a pretty shade of pink and her eyes reflected that same attraction they'd shared the night of the charity event.

He moved to the front of his desk and instead of sitting behind it, he leaned his backside against the edge, affecting a casual air. "Have a seat, please," he said, waving his hand toward the two chairs a few feet away.

"I'd rather stand, thank you," she replied, moving closer, refusing to give him a superior position.

He tipped his head at her. "So, was the weekend package not to your liking?" he asked, because that was the only reason he could think of why she was there. "I would have thought the shopping spree at Oscar de la Renta would have clinched the deal, but I'm more than willing to negotiate the terms."

In his experience, most women could be very happily incentivized by the things his money could buy. Chase honestly thought it was a generous offer, and far more pleasant than an unromantic weekend spent with him. Though she was a beautiful woman, he didn't do relationships, so he didn't think there was any reason to go on a date with her at all. Despite the fact that her willingness to stand up to him intrigued him. Not to mention, now he was curious about the kind of woman who turned down the extravagant weekend he'd offered.

Her chin lifted a fraction, and irritation flashed in her eyes. "This isn't a business transaction, and you don't get a free pass by trying to buy me off," she said, shocking him by jabbing him in his chest with her index finger to make her point. "I don't need a fancy, ridiculously expensive dress, or an extravagant spa day, or a stay at an exclusive, hoity-toity hotel. I need a goddamn date to my sister's wedding and—"

The frustration in her voice rose as she spoke, and he grabbed her wrist, cutting off her tirade before she could poke him in the chest again. He should have let go immediately, but couldn't resist caressing his thumb over that pulse point at the base of her palm, which had the interesting result of momentarily distracting her. Her lips were parted mid-sentence, and he took advantage of the interruption to speak before she did again.

"Well, that's unfortunate, because I hate weddings, and I'm not boyfriend material," he said, and finally released her hand.

He was surprised to see the fire in her eyes flicker with the barest hint of something more vulnerable. "You owe me a weekend. *You*, Chase. I won you, fair and square."

Stalemate, he thought, as he stared back at her, both of them refusing to back down.

Her gaze narrowed ever so slightly, and what appeared to be a sly smile curved her kissable lips. "Of course... I could mention to Billie that you tried to buy me off?" she asked in a challenging tone.

He groaned, because this woman had somehow managed to find his one weakness. Pleasing his half-sister. As far as Billie was concerned, Chase was slated to go on a weekend getaway with his winner sometime in the future, and he'd been fine to let her believe that ruse.

"Why is this so important to you?" he asked, crossing his arms over his chest. "That you want me, a complete stranger, to accompany you to your sister's wedding?"

She glanced away and exhaled a deep breath, shedding more of that earlier bravado. When she met his gaze again, she drew him in with her now open and earnest expression. "Because my sister is marrying my ex, and I don't want to show up alone and endure looks of pity from the guests," she revealed.

Shock rippled through him. That was the last reason he would have expected, and he could see how much that confession had cost her by the pained look in her eyes. Despite wanting to remain unaffected, he found he wasn't immune to this vulnerable side she'd given him a glimpse of, because it was *real*.

"And technically, you aren't a stranger, because my parents think we've been dating for a while now," she added with a smirk. "I've already told my family all about you, Chase Gossard, and that I'm bringing you home for the weekend. So, yeah, *that's* why I bought a bachelor, and now it has to be you who takes me."

He dragged a hand along his jaw and swore beneath his breath, knowing he'd be a real asshole to refuse after hearing how personal this was for her. "Fucking great," he muttered.

She tipped her head to the side, regarding him curiously. "Why did you agree to do the bachelor auction for Billie if you had no intentions of following through?"

It was a fair question, but his reasons were personal and private and between himself and his half-sister. "I *thought* I'd followed through spectacularly," he said in a droll tone, then shook his head. "Do you know how many women would kill for the kind of weekend I offered you?"

She shrugged, causing his traitorous gaze to drop to the rise and fall of her breasts beneath her silky blouse. "I'm not just any woman."

"Clearly," he said, realizing she was the complete opposite. An anomaly for him when he was used to females expecting those lavish things his money could buy.

"Answer my question," she said softly, refusing to let him off so easy. "Why did you agree to do the bachelor auction for Billie if you had no intention of following through?"

Her pretty eyes stared directly into his, and he

shifted his backside against the desk, bracing his hands on the edge in order to resist the insane urge to grip her hips and pull her forward. Toward him, until her figure molded against his—just to feel how her curves aligned against his body. Everything about her was so authentic and natural, from her full lips and those freckles across the bridge of her nose and cheeks, to her small but firm breasts, to the perfect swell of her hips. She didn't rely on collagen, or silicone, or any artificial enhancements to amplify her beauty and he found that incredibly refreshing and attractive.

She was waiting patiently for him to reply. Considering how open and honest she'd been about her own uncomfortable predicament, and how genuinely caring she seemed about his answer, he decided to share a part of himself he normally wouldn't.

"I agreed to stand in as a replacement bachelor because Billie rarely asks me for anything." Of course, his reasons went a helluva lot deeper than that superficial explanation, but divulging even that much of his relationship with his half-sister with anyone was huge.

"And..." He exhaled a breath and opted for even more honesty here. "I guess I just didn't think through the whole 'weekend' thing, and spending it with one woman. I don't date. I'm not... personable and charming or one to show a woman a good time outside of the bedroom," he said, giving her his own smirk in return. "And I'm self-aware enough to know it's wrong to lead any woman into thinking I'm something that I'm not, or that I'll give them more than just… companionship for a night or two."

Her brows rose, and he didn't miss the awareness swirling in the depths of her eyes. "Well, at least you're honest. But that doesn't let you off the hook. You weren't my first choice of a bachelor, but I'm stuck with you, so I'd appreciate it if you'd accompany me to my sister's wedding."

She said it with a soft, teasing smile, the earlier tension between them all but dissipated, and damn if that playful look on her face didn't make his own defenses crumble a bit—what the hell was up with that? When she'd walked into his office, he'd been so adamant about doing whatever it took not to spend a weekend with her, and now, after learning she was trying to save face at her sister's wedding to her ex, his attitude had shifted.

It was true that he didn't want to disappoint Billie if she discovered he hadn't followed through on what was expected of him, but he realized that he also didn't want to let Lauren down, either, because shockingly, he genuinely liked her. And it didn't hurt that there was true chemistry between them, which couldn't be said for the other women he'd dated lately.

As he'd said, he wasn't anyone's knight in shining armor, but Lauren wasn't asking him to be one. She just didn't want to show up to an unpleasant situation alone, which he could understand. Playing her pretend boyfriend was a simple enough thing to do. It was one weekend out of his life, and then he could consider his obligation to Billie, and to the Future Fast Track bachelor auction, and Lauren, paid in full.

"Okay, I'll grant you your weekend and play the part of your boyfriend," he said, doing his best to dedicate himself to the ruse, even if it was something outside of his comfort zone. He wasn't a man who half-assed anything once he committed himself. "Where do we go from here?"

Her shoulders fell, her relief nearly palpable. "The wedding isn't until next month, so we have a few weeks to figure out the specifics. Why don't we set a day and time to meet up and discuss things more in detail?" she suggested. "Maybe get to know each other a little better so we can sell the whole relationship thing and we don't look like two total strangers who just met?"

He nodded in agreement and did a quick mental rundown of his schedule. He had a business dinner this Saturday with an out-of-town client, but he was free the following weekend. "How about dinner at my place next Saturday?"

Her eyes widened in surprise. "Your place?"

He shrugged. "I figure we'll both need time to learn some things about each other to make this fake relationship look authentic. We'll have more privacy at my apartment, we can take whatever time we need, and we don't have to worry about anyone listening in to our conversation."

A pleased smile curved her lips. "Okay, next Saturday it is."

He pulled his cell phone from the front pocket of

his slacks and used his fingerprint to unlock the screen. "What's your number? I'll text you from my personal phone so you can reach me directly, instead of going through my assistant."

She flashed him a cheeky grin. "Well, now I feel special."

An unexpected chuckle escaped him before he could stop it. "You should."

Her grin remained as she rattled off her number, and he shot her a quick text message so that she now had his. As soon as he tucked his phone back into his pocket, she stepped right up to him and enveloped him in a hug before he realized her intent.

Shocked by the warm and endearing gesture because he was unused to that kind of open display of affection outside of Billie, he felt his body stiffen as she wrapped her arms around his waist, pressing all those sensual curves right up against him as he'd envisioned only minutes before. He forced himself to relax, and tentatively, his own hands slid around her waist, instinctively returning the hug.

Or maybe he just selfishly wanted to be close to her, to soak up her vivacious, accepting personality, despite his attempts to keep his guard up. His hand slipped down to the slight indentation at the base of her spine, much lower than was probably appropriate, and he inhaled a deep breath. God, everything about her was so warm and soft and fragrant. Heat shot through his veins, along with something far more intimate. The lust and desire was a given, but the *connection* he felt in that moment with Lauren was unprecedented and threw his equilibrium off-kilter.

The embrace only lasted a few seconds before she released him and stepped back. "Sorry, I'm a hugger," she said impishly, clearly having sensed his initial discomfort. "But you need to get used to being touchy-feely with me, if we want to make *us* look believable to my family."

She'd put him through such a range of emotions in such a short span of time, and his head was still spinning from that embrace, that all he could manage was a grunt as a response.

She laughed softly, as if understanding. "Thank you for doing this for me, Chase."

He cleared his throat and found his voice. "You didn't give me much of a choice, did you?" he said, injecting a bit of humor in his tone.

Despite everything he'd put her through, Lauren's eyes held a mischievous little sparkle. "You still could have said no, or made some excuse not to do it, but you didn't. You'd better be careful, or else I'm going to think you're actually a really nice guy beneath that grumpy façade of yours."

With that sassy retort, she turned around and walked out of his office, leaving him with the tantalizing view of her hips swaying and her firm ass outlined in her fitted black pants… making him wonder what the hell he'd gotten himself into.

Chapter Four

"SO, I THINK this is the last of the items left from the charity event," Lauren said the following week, when Billie came by the Meridian to collect a box filled with Future Fast Track signs, posters, and other unused paper goods. "I could have had it couriered over to your office, instead of you coming by to pick it up."

Billie grinned unabashedly. "I know, but if I'm being completely honest... I'm nosey and wanted to know what's going on with you and Chase."

Lauren paused for a moment. She wasn't sure what Billie knew about any of her interactions with Chase and didn't want to assume anything. "What do you mean?"

She chewed on her lower lip, her eyes glimmering with a hint of worry behind her black framed glasses. "Has he been in touch about how you'll spend your weekend together?"

Throwing Chase under the bus by telling his half-sister that he'd initially tried to buy her off with an all-expense-paid weekend *without* him wouldn't serve any purpose other than to disappoint Billie. Clearly, she adored her brother, despite his uptight personality, and all that mattered to Lauren was that he'd agreed to be her date to her sister's wedding.

"So, you haven't talked to him since the charity event?" Lauren asked instead.

Billie shook her head and absently ran her fingers along the edge of the cardboard box holding the nonprofit's things. "I definitely thought about asking him, but I know my closed-off brother and knew I'd get a straighter answer from you, most likely. I mean, he made it pretty obvious up on that stage that being auctioned off was equivalent to having a root canal, and I'm just hoping that he didn't totally turn you off with his brusque attitude."

"Oh, he tried," she admitted, and found herself grinning as she recalled her initial interaction with Chase at his office, and his unsuccessful attempts to dissuade her. "But we came to an understanding."

"Yeah, I know he can be a little gruff," Billie said with a wince. "Do you mind me asking... why did you bid on Chase, anyway?"

"Because I need a date to my sister's wedding next month in Massachusetts and he was my last resort. *Literally,*" she added wryly. "I was expecting to bid on Neil Pierson."

Billie's eyes grew wide with shock. "Wow, he actually agreed to accompany you to a wedding for an *entire* weekend?"

Lauren laughed at the disbelief she heard in the other woman's voice. "It took some convincing, but yes."

"I'm glad you gave him a chance," Billie said, her tone heartfelt, showing just how much she cared for her brother. "I know Chase has this whole standoffish vibe going on, but underneath that cantankerous demeanor, he's really a solid, decent guy."

"I know," Lauren said, realizing she meant it. Because despite Chase's initial reluctance, he *had* responded to how open—and yes, even vulnerable—she'd been with him about her situation, when a man without a heart would have still refused to fulfill his obligation. She'd also seen that soft spot he had for Billie, which spoke volumes, too.

"I'm actually glad you won him," Billie admitted softly.

Lauren blinked at the other woman. "You are?"

She nodded and smiled. "I think you'll be good for Chase."

"In what way?" Lauren couldn't help but be skeptical.

Billie absently tucked a strand of pink hair behind her ear and shrugged. "You're not like the other shallow, superficial women he dates, which I know he does on purpose. It makes it easier for him to suppress his emotions and keep his distance."

"Why?" Lauren asked, intrigued by this deeper insight to Chase.

"It's… complicated." Billie paused for a moment, as if trying to decide what to reveal. "I think he harbors a lot of anger over what our mother, Darlene, did to his father, and how she left Chase when he was just a young boy," Billie said, her tone tinged with sadness. "And there's definitely lingering resentment toward his dad, who kept things from Chase until his father was literally on his deathbed a few years ago, like the fact that I even existed."

Lauren's heart clenched in her chest. She couldn't imagine how painful that revelation had been for Chase, not to mention being abandoned by his own mother.

"Anyway, the things he'd had to deal with..." Billie's voice trailed off and she shook her head, as if realizing how much she'd divulged. "I'm just letting you know that Chase has valid reasons for his walls, for not letting people in or getting too close, and I would love to see him loosen up and enjoy life beyond work. I just want him to be happy. *Really* happy, you know? And you've got such a great attitude in general, you're so upbeat and positive, how can he not respond to that?"

Clearly, this man had many layers, and while she appreciated the insight to his psyche, which explained a lot of his behavior, the last thing she wanted was for Billie to pin her hopes on Lauren, thinking she could magically cure Chase of a life that had clearly been filled with pain and disappointments.

"I'm not looking to fix him," she said, though a part of her wished she had the ability to do so.

"I'm sorry," Billie immediately apologized. "I didn't mean it that way. I know that nobody is responsible for fixing Chase and his suppressed issues and emotions except Chase himself." Then, she smiled as she picked up the box of things Lauren had packed up for her. "But I can't deny the thought of you shaking up his nice, orderly world doesn't give me a bit of hope that maybe, hopefully, he'll walk away from this experience a better man who smiles more and frowns a whole lot less."

Lauren laughed, because that was a lot to wish for with a staid man like Chase, and her own powers of persuasion only went so far. It was going to be difficult enough to wipe that perpetual scowl off his face when he met her family. "I offer no guarantees."

Lauren walked Billie to the elevator and once the other woman was gone, she returned to her office to finish an event contract she'd been working on for a client. Except the legalese kept blurring on the screen as her mind kept replaying what Billie had told her about Chase and his reasons for being so guarded. A few sentences, really, and most of it vague, but it had been enough to pique Lauren's curiosity.

The man was such an enigma, and as unwise as it might be, she wanted to know more about him. She wanted to peel away those protective layers and soothe the hurt beneath, which was dangerous, because she suspected he wouldn't appreciate anyone poking around and stirring up all those complicated emotions he obviously kept on lockdown. But damn if she didn't want to try, because Chase Gossard was a paradox who intrigued her. On one hand, imposing and intimidating, and on the other, a man who'd been surprisingly compassionate and empathetic to her situation. He'd lowered all those defenses and reservations enough to give Lauren something important to *her*.

Which said a lot about the kind of man he truly was.

She thought about that spontaneous hug she'd given him that day at his office to express her gratitude, and how stiff and hesitant he'd been at first. It had been a quick embrace, but she'd been hyperaware of him the entire time, of his big, warm hands on her lower back and the heat of his solid, muscular body flush against hers. There was no denying the mutual desire that had flashed between them before she'd ended the hug.

One thing was for certain. There was nothing fake about the attraction and chemistry between them, which would at least go a long way in convincing her family that she and Chase were a couple. And for her quick weekend trip home, that was all she needed.

Chapter Five

A S PLANNED, THE following Saturday evening, Lauren took an Uber to the address Chase had texted her, to a building in Manhattan's Flatiron District, where he lived. After the driver dropped her off, she headed inside the upscale lobby and checked in with the doorman. Chase had already informed him she'd be arriving and he sent her up.

Since the elevator required a key card, the doorman used his. He punched the number for Chase's floor, and she made the ride up alone, acutely aware of just how wealthy Chase had to be to live in not only this area of the city, but in this condominium. Even the air she breathed smelled like money.

He'd modestly referred to his place as an "apartment", but as the doors slid open and she stepped directly into a foyer, which in turn led to a spacious living area that flowed into a ridiculously large chef's kitchen, she recategorized his home as a *penthouse*. She'd known he was wealthy, but as she took in the massive floor plan and the unfettered view of the Flatiron District, the term *filthy rich* came to mind.

Lauren set her purse on the coffee table, knowing

she was probably gawking, but she found herself awed by the wide-open views of the city and walls of windows that added a sense of space and light. Double doors opened out onto a terrace with potted plants and a sitting area, and while the October evening had a bit of a chill in the air, the lit gas firepit outside promised coziness and warmth.

The interior décor was just as understated as the man himself, painted and furnished in bright whites and grays, with a touch of navy blue here and there, and state-of-the-art finishes throughout. Modern conceptual pieces of artwork hung on the walls, but overall the place was uncluttered and tastefully designed.

"I see you found the place okay," Chase said, snapping Lauren out of her awestruck moment.

"I did," she replied, and followed the sound of his voice to the jaw-dropping kitchen, which was equipped with top-of-the-line stainless steel appliances, including one of those fancy French door refrigerators, a double oven, and an indoor grill. The countertops were a dark gray quartz, matching the obscenely large work island in the room.

And then there was the man himself standing on the other side of the counter, wearing a deep gray Henley and a pair of dark denim jeans—both no doubt designer brands because she couldn't imagine a man like Chase purchasing anything from a mid-range department store. Her eyes were drawn to the way he'd pushed up the sleeves of his shirt, exposing his strong forearms, as he uncorked a bottle of wine, before traveling up to his face. Though his hair was a bit disheveled, like he'd been running his fingers through the strands, his jaw was smooth and clean shaven and she caught a hint of his enticing cologne in the air.

She was used to seeing him in expensive tailored suits, but she couldn't deny that he looked equally hot in this more casual attire. He was always so well put together, exuding confidence and a sense of authority despite what he wore.

In comparison, she felt a bit frumpy in her own choice of clothing. She hadn't wanted him to think she was trying to dress to impress him, and had opted for comfort over style. She'd chosen her favorite purple and well-worn light sweater top and a pair of soft, faded jeans. She'd pulled her hair back into a ponytail, and since she wasn't much of a makeup girl on the weekends, she'd only used tinted moisturizer, a bit of mascara, and lip gloss.

But the way his gaze darkened as he looked at her caused a seductive heat to swirl in her belly, and her very neglected pussy clenched with that ever-present awareness that simmered between them.

She cleared her throat, and ignoring the warmth suffusing her cheeks, she walked more fully into the kitchen and toward him, inhaling the delicious scent of something savory. "This is an impressive setup," she said, complimenting his culinary space as she ran a hand over the smooth quartz countertop. "Do you like to cook?"

"Not particularly," he said in a wry tone as he poured two glasses of the red wine before handing her one. "But my chef enjoys having the space to spread out while he's cooking and prepping my meals for the week."

Of course he had a personal chef, she thought as she took a sip of the smooth and flavorful pinot noir. She felt slightly overwhelmed by all his wealth and conveniences compared to how modestly she'd grown up—and even where and how she currently lived. Then again, after reading as many articles as she'd been able to find on Chase Gossard on the internet, she got the impression he was a self-made man and didn't necessarily have all these luxuries growing up, either. She supposed if she had the money, she'd enjoy the finer things in life, too.

"How about you? Do you enjoy cooking?" he asked, leaning a hip against the counter before shocking her with a rare and sexy grin. "For the sake of getting to know you better, of course."

"Yes, I love to cook," she replied, warming to the subject. "I grew up in a small town, where my parents still live, and while there are a few family-owned restaurants, we couldn't really afford to eat out very often. All our meals were home-cooked and made from scratch, which I can appreciate more as an adult," she said with a light laugh. "Unfortunately, I don't get to do that kind of cooking in my tiny apartment, but I do miss baking and making those home-cooked comfort meals that are my favorites."

"Like what?" he asked, genuine interest in his eyes.

She thought of some of the dinners she'd enjoyed the most. "Like chicken and dumplings, shepherd's pie, chicken fried steak, and fresh buttered green beans picked right from our very own garden, where we grew most of our fruits and vegetables."

"Sounds very... Mayberry," he said, surprising her by using the term coined by an old TV show that referenced an idyllic and picturesque fictional town.

Which wasn't far from the truth, she mused, complete with busybodies who liked to be in everyone's business. "What do you know about Mayberry, city boy?"

He shrugged. "My father used to watch reruns of *The Andy Griffith Show*."

"So did my gramps, right along with *Gunsmoke*. I used to love watching those programs with him and wanted to be just like the saloon proprietor Miss Kitty when I grew up, and I was secretly in love with Marshal Dillon," she said, grinning at the fond, but silly recollection. "Did you watch those shows with your dad?"

"I didn't have much of a choice."

Chase's tone was surprisingly gruff, telling her that it wasn't a pleasant memory for him. Based on the small bit of information Billie had revealed, Lauren knew his father was a touchy subject. And as much as she wanted to ask about their relationship, the way Chase abruptly turned away to open the double oven to retrieve their dinner told her he probably wasn't in a sharing mood when it came to his dad.

Instead, she watched him grab some pot holders and remove one of the two casserole dishes from the oven to set on the small dining table adjacent to the kitchen, then he did the same for the smaller, second dish.

"I hope you're hungry," he said as she joined him at the table, bringing both of their glasses of wine with her. "Marcus made us chicken marsala and risotto."

Chase had been kind enough to ask her if she had any dietary restrictions, of which she had none, and she loved Italian food. The savory, delectable scent of dinner almost made her groan, but she wasn't able to hold back the loud growl of her stomach, a reminder that she'd skipped lunch that day.

He chuckled as they each took a seat. "I'll take that as a yes."

"I'm starved and this looks and smells fantastic," she said, spreading her napkin on her lap. "My compliments to the chef."

"I'll be sure to pass them on to Marcus. He'll be pleased that he managed to impress you." He reached for the chicken marsala and added a portion to her plate, then his own, followed by the risotto.

They started in on the meal, and after a few delicious bites, Chase spoke.

"So, tell me what I need to know about your family and what to expect when I meet them," he said.

She appreciated him initiating the conversation.

Talking about her family was an easy enough topic for her to warm up to, and after finishing her bite of chicken, she gave him a quick rundown. "Well, my parents, Dale and Penny, have been happily married for almost thirty-one years, and have lived their entire lives in Fairview, which is a small town about ten miles outside of Springfield, Massachusetts," she said, pausing to take a sip of her wine before continuing. "I only have one sibling, my sister, Ashley, who is the one getting married."

He nodded. "And what about your grandparents? Are they still around?"

She'd been expecting him to ask about Ashley being involved with her ex, but he surprised her by not broaching that subject yet. At some point she'd have to give him the details so he understood the situation, but she was grateful to talk about something else while they ate.

"My grandparents on my father's side have both passed, along with my grandma on my mother's side. But my gramps is still going strong at eighty-three, though he did just recently have a stroke."

Chase met her gaze, his own kind and caring. "Is he going to be okay?"

"Yeah, he's pretty damn tough." Despite knowing that her gramps was good, she still felt a lump form in her throat that she had to swallow back. "I adore him, honestly. Ever since I was a little girl, we've been super close, and growing up I used to spend all my free time on my grandparents' farm."

"Your sister, too?" he asked.

She shook her head and cast a glance at Chase, who was still eating his dinner, but his attention was focused on her and what she was telling him. "My sister and I were complete opposites and we didn't spend much time together. She was the beauty queen and I was the tomboy. She liked frilly dresses, dolls, and tea parties, and I loved fishing with Gramps, riding horses, milking cows, and collecting eggs from the hen house. More times than not, I came home *smelling* like a farm, with muck all over my clothes, which my sister hated. Ashley grew up in the pageant circuit, always immaculately dressed and perfectly put together, while I went rock climbing and rode my bike through the mud and wore my scrapes and bruises like a badge of honor."

He chuckled in amusement, which was the last thing she'd expected him to do when she'd just painted a very vivid picture of how different she and her sister were. And how Ashley was clearly the more glamorous of the two of them.

"Damn," he said, placing his fork on his empty plate. "So, you've always been feisty and independent, and basically not giving a shit what others think?"

She secretly loved *that's* what he'd taken away from what she'd divulged, and found herself grinning. "Go ahead and add stubborn and determined to the mix, too."

He smirked. "Oh, yeah, I saw that for myself firsthand."

It wasn't a dig or said with criticism, which told her how far they'd come in such a very short time since the evening she'd purchased him at the bachelor auction, then their confrontation in his office. He was so much more relaxed now, and while she sensed that he was still very emotionally guarded, there was no more strain between them, or with their conversation.

She decided to take advantage of that and switched the spotlight onto Chase, eager to learn more about him.

"Okay, your turn to give me the rundown on your family."

She didn't miss the way he visibly tensed, or the way he shifted uncomfortably in his seat before he responded in a cool tone. "There's not much to tell. Both of my parents are gone, and you know that Billie is my half-sister. That's the extent of my family."

His reply didn't invite further discussion, but that didn't stop her from prying a bit more. "Did you have a close relationship with your parents?"

He laughed bitterly. "No."

End of conversation, his tone said, but hadn't they just agreed that she was stubborn and determined? Chase was clearly a man who held his cards close, but Billie had given her enough bits and pieces about this man to pique her interest. He was such an enigma, and she found herself wanting to know everything about him and what had happened in his past to mold him into the man he was today. One who didn't let other people in, or too close, according to Billie.

She knew what she was about to ask was risky, but she did it anyway. "Earlier, when I asked if you watched *The Andy Griffith Show* and *Gunsmoke* with your dad, what did you mean when you said that you didn't have much of a choice?"

His jaw clenched and his fingers tightened on the stem of his wineglass, as if she'd hit some kind of nerve. He turned his head, and when he met her gaze, there was unmistakable anger glimmering there—at her for prodding, or at the memories she was forcing him to relive, she wasn't sure.

Finally, he spoke. "Unlike you, I didn't have a charmed childhood," he said, and while his words were blunt, his tone wasn't hurtful or mean, but rather painfully honest. "My mother left my father and me when I was seven years old and ran off with another man. And my father stopped giving a damn about anything after that, including me. He fell into a dark depression. He lost his job and sat in his recliner drinking beer all fucking day long feeling sorry for himself, and yes, he watched those shows over and over and over. That's *all* we fucking did."

With every little bit he revealed, Lauren's chest ached with sadness and sorrow for the little boy Chase had been. That those awful memories were all he had to look back on. She already knew he wasn't a demonstrative man after that hug she'd given him in his office, but that didn't stop her from wanting to climb onto his lap and wrap her arms around him, to tell him that it was okay to be angry that his father had abandoned him, just as much as his mother had. And to let him know that he wasn't alone, that despite only knowing him a short while, she cared about him.

But she stayed in her seat and she didn't reach out and touch him, either, like she wanted to do.

After a long moment passed, he exhaled a deep breath and pressed his fingers against the bridge of his nose. "Sorry," he muttered, then dropped his hand and met her gaze again, seemingly calmer now. "The last thing I want to do is talk about my parents. As far as your family is concerned, they only need to know that they've both died and I have one sibling, Billie."

"Okay," she said softly, respecting his wishes.

He abruptly stood up and since they were done with their dinner, he started collecting their plates and silverware. "Why don't you go out to the terrace and sit by the fire while I clean up the kitchen and put the food away."

She stood, too. "Can I at least help you clear the table?"

He shook his head. "No, I've got it, and I could use a few minutes to myself, if you don't mind."

There was nothing harsh about the tone of his request, but knowing what a private, reserved man Chase was, she understood his need for space to regain his composure. "Of course."

He managed a small, appreciative smile. "Marcus made cannolis for dessert. How about I bring you a few with some coffee? I can add Baileys in it, if you'd like?"

"I would love that." The last thing she'd ever turn down was dessert.

"And then we can talk about your sister, and your ex," he said, taking the dishes to the sink.

"Now there's a fun conversation," she joked, but knew it had to be done. While Chase's past was clearly off limits, hers was going to be blatantly in their faces for the weekend, and he needed to be prepared.

"By the way," he said, stopping her before she could walk out to the terrace. "Where are we staying while we're there?" He grimaced. "Please don't tell me we're staying with your parents."

She laughed. "No, that would be extremely awkward," she assured him. "I know staying at the house would be my mother's preference, but once I moved out she made my room into a sewing and crafting area, and my sister Ashley's room is now where my gramps stays. I'll make reservations for us at the bed-and-breakfast in town."

"I'll pay for it, and any other expenses," he insisted. "Call Victoria with the information and she'll get it taken care of."

Lauren wasn't going to argue. "Okay. Thank you."

Even though she really wanted to help Chase with the cleanup, she headed out onto the terrace and sat on the outdoor couch situated around the lit firepit, instead of one of the single chairs. The low flames chased away most of the chill in the October air, but she still grabbed the lightweight blanket draped over a cushion and spread it out over her legs.

She glanced back toward the condo, seeing into the kitchen through the bank of windows. Chase was standing at the island putting the leftovers into containers. There was a slight crease between his brows, but the earlier anger she'd provoked with her question about his father was gone, thank goodness.

At least he wasn't holding her curiosity against her, and really, for the most part he'd been very pleasant and amiable. Likeable, even, as shocking as that was when she remembered the gruff and grumpy man she'd met at the bachelor auction.

Lauren found herself smiling as she continued to watch Chase as he made two cups of coffee and plated a few cannolis, remembering her conversation with Billie. She'd told the other woman that she wasn't looking to fix Chase and his issues, and that still held true. However, in that moment Lauren decided she was going to give Billie her other wish, to shake up her brother's neat and orderly world and get him to loosen up and relax during their time together.

Going home for her sister's wedding was undoubtedly going to be difficult for various reasons, but why not enjoy her time with Chase, and vice versa? There was no denying their mutual attraction, so there was no reason why they couldn't indulge in a little no-strings-attached side benefit to their arrangement, right?

She just needed to see if he was game.

Chapter Six

C HASE ADDED BAILEYS to the two mugs of coffee on the counter, grateful for the short time he had alone in the kitchen to recenter his mind and emotions after Lauren had shifted their conversation to his father, which was always a touchy subject for him. He didn't discuss that part of his past with anyone, *ever*. The day his dad died was the day Chase swore he'd keep those terrible and painful memories locked up in the past, where they belonged.

But leave it to the persistent woman sitting out on his terrace to press the issue. She'd been nice about her inquiry, but her question had been equivalent to her shaking up a bottle of champagne (him), to the point that all that pressure he'd been suppressing for so many years had popped the cork he'd shoved into the bottle, and his anger had flared. He'd only told her a small fraction about his past, but there had been a moment when he'd wanted to spill *everything*, just to release all the bitterness and resentment festering deep inside.

He hated that he'd lost his composure when he was a man so in control of his emotions. Most of the women he'd dated would have been insulted or hurt that he'd snapped at them, but not Lauren. No, this woman wasn't offended by much, and knowing he didn't have to put on any pretenses with her made him feel relieved, and too damned comfortable around her. Which was why he'd probably allowed himself to slip and say *anything* about his relationship with his father.

He exhaled a deep breath and grabbing the two mug handles with one hand, and the plate with the dessert in the other, he walked out onto the terrace. Lauren watched him approach with a smile that soothed the last frayed edges of his emotions. He set the coffees and cannolis on the stone table built around the firepit, then took a seat next to her on the couch.

He handed one mug to her, then took the other for himself, waiting while she took a drink of the Baileys-infused coffee before broaching the subject of her ex marrying her sister.

And yeah, he was well aware that it made him a hypocrite that he was about to make her talk about *her* past, but she didn't have much of a choice if she wanted him in the loop of what happened between her and her ex. And, if he was being honest with himself, he was curious to know what idiot would let a woman like Lauren go, then turn around and backstab her by hooking up with her sister. Totally fucking classless, in his opinion.

"So, tell me about your sister's situation with your ex, so I'm aware," he said.

She scrunched her freckled nose, as if she were about to discuss something distasteful. "I guess explaining things from the beginning would help. My ex, Greg, is one of the veterinarians in town and I worked as the front-end manager of the place. We also pretty much grew up together, considering what a small town Fairview is." She took another drink of her coffee. "Anyway, we dated for about a year, then got engaged. It was just how things worked in such a small town," she said with a shrug.

She put her mug down and pulled the blanket higher up on her lap before continuing, her gaze on the firepit's flames. "My sister also worked at the vet's, helping to take care of the animals while they were kenneled for the day, or a few days if they had surgery and were recovering. One evening, after I'd left the office for the afternoon, Greg called to tell me that there was an emergency surgery on a dog that came in and he was going to be a few hours late. So, I thought I'd take him dinner."

Chase inwardly cringed, already sensing where this story was heading.

She shifted her gaze back to him, a wry look in her eyes. "There was no emergency surgery. Instead, I found Greg and Ashley in his office, going at it pretty hot and heavy until I cleared my throat and interrupted them."

Shock at her calm response rippled through him, when most scorned women would have gone ballistic and thrown dinner at them, or worse. "That's all you did?" he asked incredulously. "Just cleared your throat?"

She laughed lightly. "Shockingly, finding them in that passionate embrace didn't devastate me, and I saw no reason to yell and scream and make a scene. So, I put the dinner on his desk along with my engagement ring while my sister was trying to straighten her blouse and refasten her bra, and then I left while Greg was sputtering out an apology."

Of course, Lauren would be the bigger person. "You weren't... upset?"

"I think I was more disappointed, and even relieved, which told me a lot about my true feelings for Greg," she said with a shrug. "And that marrying him would have been a huge mistake."

He couldn't detect any real pain or hurt, which was good because Chase was starting to feel protective of Lauren. And he didn't want to have to kick the groom's ass when Chase met him.

"That doesn't excuse the fact that they were messing around behind your back," he said, stunned by the heated tone of his own voice.

"No, it doesn't," she agreed, absently pleating the blanket between her fingers. "Honestly, it wasn't the affair that was humiliating, because to this day no one in town knows what transpired that night at the office, but only what happened *after* that day."

He almost hated to ask. "Which was?"

She shifted on the couch, turning her body more toward his, bringing them in closer proximity. "Clearly, when I walked out of Greg's office, we were done. That was a given, but everyone in town just assumed that Greg ended things with *me*, not knowing what I'd walked in on."

He tried to wrap his mind around what she'd just said. "And what about your parents? Do they know the truth?"

"Yes, I told them," she said, her tone layered with sadness. "They were obviously upset on my behalf, but considering Ashley is their daughter, too, they were torn. Of course they supported me, but they weren't going to disown Ashley, either, and I didn't expect them to. I mean, I could have made the truth be known to *everyone*, but the last thing I wanted was to cause even more drama, or make things even more uncomfortable within the family, or have everyone in the town label Ashley as *the other woman*, even though she was. I'm not the spiteful type, and it was just easier to let everyone believe the lie, except…"

He heard the hitch in her voice as that last word trailed off, and he was too invested in the story, *in her*, not to know what had caused that emotional falter. "Except what?"

Her lips pursed. "Except when Greg and Ashley started openly dating a week later, I became fodder for town gossip."

"How so?" he asked, setting his coffee mug next to hers on the firepit table.

She bit her bottom lip before answering. "Because Greg had chosen the beautiful beauty pageant sister, over the plain-Jane tomboy sibling. Truthfully, out of everything that happened, the looks of pity from the people in town were the most painful to endure."

He swore beneath his breath. Yet endure it, she had, to keep the peace in the family. "Is there animosity between you and your sister?"

"No, not really," she said softly. "But we were never really close to begin with, as I'd told you earlier. We've never even talked about what happened. And yes, the few times I've been home it has been awkward between us, and she's done her best to keep any interactions between us to a minimum, which of course everyone thinks is because, again, I was the one who got dumped and they feel sorry for me."

She exhaled a deep sigh and met his gaze. "You know, as hurt as I was about the situation, I can live with the fact that it happened, because I don't think it was vindictive on either Greg's or Ashley's part. *But*, it would have been nice if my sister had apologized, instead of always avoiding the big elephant in the room when we're together."

He winced, unable to imagine how uncomfortable that had to be for Lauren. And unfair, too.

"I know my parents and Gramps have worried about me since the breakup, and as much as I've promised them that I'm okay, I'm not sure they really believe it," she went on. "So, that's another reason why I wanted to bring a 'boyfriend' home for the wedding. That hopefully *seeing* for themselves that I'm happy and that I've moved on with someone else will ease their concerns. All I really want is for things to be normal and not have that one incident hanging over us for the rest of our lives. I don't think I'll ever have a close relationship with Ashley, but I want to keep things in the family copacetic."

As she opened up and shared the painful details, Chase couldn't help but feel empathy toward Lauren, and the entire situation. Now he had a much clearer understanding of why she'd bought him at the bachelor auction. Not just to keep any attention on her being single and alone to a minimum, but to alleviate her parents' worries, as well.

"The way things happened wasn't ideal, and I would have appreciated not being blindsided by their affair," she went on. "But honestly, the breakup was the push I needed to leave Fairview and pursue my dreams."

The smile that curved her lips now lit up her eyes, too. "I've always wanted to live in a big city and be an event planner like I am at the Meridian, and I'm genuinely happy here in New York, more than I ever was in Fairview. The whole thing with my sister and Greg was really a blessing in disguise, because looking back, I know for certain I would have been miserable being married to him. At least I saw real passion between him and Ashley that night at the office. I couldn't remember a time that Greg was nearly tearing my clothes off to have his way with me."

"That's on him, not on you," Chase said vehemently, because obviously her ex was an idiot.

"I think that lack of passion was on both of us, because I had no urge to tear his clothes off, either. Sex between us was always just… bland and boring, if I'm being honest. I always wanted something more…" As if realizing what she'd been about to reveal, her cheeks pinkened, and she ducked her head in embarrassment. "And now that I've probably given you more information than you ever wanted to know about my sex life, I think I'll have a cannoli."

He watched her reach for the dessert, oddly charmed by that rare blush on her face, and what she'd been about to divulge. "There's nothing wrong with wanting something *more*," he said, his voice low and husky.

She'd just taken a bite of the sweet ricotta-filled pastry, and her pretty eyes suddenly danced with humor as she chewed, then swallowed. "Why, Mr. Gossard, are you *offering* something more?" she asked flirtatiously.

He felt the breath leave his lungs, because in that moment he had the urge to press her back onto the small couch and show her the kind of passion he could ignite between the two of them. He wanted to swipe his tongue along her bottom lip and lick off the light coating of powdered sugar lingering there, before plundering deeper. He wanted to strip off her sweater and bra and see if her nipples tasted just as sweet before letting his mouth traverse down between her thighs for yet another sample, until she was delirious with pleasure and learned the true meaning of ecstasy.

Fuck. He shifted in his seat as desire shot straight to his dick. All evening long, he'd tried his best to ignore the heated attraction that had been evident between them since day one, and Jesus, now it was all he could do to keep from answering her question with an unequivocal and enthusiastic *yes.*

He cleared his throat and somehow managed to be a gentleman, and instead tortured himself as he watched her slowly suck the powdered sugar from her fingers after finishing her cannoli. Slowly, deliberately, thoroughly…

"I just mean, *you* deserve more," he said, desperate to distract his brain from envisioning his aching cock replacing her fingers as they slid into her mouth and her lips and tongue wrapped sensually around them. "More passion. More lust-fueled encounters. More wild, uninhibited sex."

Amusement sparkled in her eyes and an alluring smile curved her lips as she leaned much closer, drawing his gaze to that mouth he wanted to kiss and devour. "I do deserve all those things, don't I?" she agreed, her voice low and sultry.

What. The. Hell. He was suddenly dealing with a vixen, a woman who was clearly seducing him. If it had been any other random female, he would have dove right in and wouldn't have thought twice about slaking his needs before sending her on her way, without any intention of ever seeing her again, as was his method of operation.

But the last thing Chase wanted to do was take advantage of *this* woman, who deserved more romance and finesse than a one-night stand, which was all he was good for. Great sex, for sure, but no promises or commitment to go with it, and he respected Lauren enough not to cross that line with her. He wasn't emotionally equipped to be anything more than her temporary, stand-in boyfriend for a weekend.

Telling himself he was doing the right thing, he abruptly stood and reached for the dessert plate. "How about I wrap up the extra cannoli for you to take home?" he said, then beelined it back into the kitchen so he could fucking breathe without wanting to pounce on Lauren.

Pulling tin foil from a drawer, he ripped off a sheet much too aggressively, thanks to all the pent-up desire waging war inside of him. Forcing himself to exhale a deep breath and calm the fuck down, he wrapped up the pastries more gently so he didn't crush them to pieces, just as he caught sight of Lauren heading back inside. Feigning indifference, he leaned his backside against the counter and waited for her to join him.

Her ponytail bounced with every purposeful step, and he recognized that determined expression on her face, the one Chase knew from experience didn't bode well for him. Not when she walked right up to where he was and literally stood toe to toe with him, leaving him no means of escape. She was so close she had to tip her head back to look up at him, but when she did, there was no mistaking the unwavering tenacity shining in her eyes.

"You wanted to kiss me out on the terrace," she said, just like a statement of fact, which it was. "Why didn't you?"

He swallowed back a groan. His hands fisted at his sides to keep from grabbing her, and the truth tumbled out before he could stop it. "Because you, Lauren Connelly, tempt me beyond all reason," he said, the words coming out on a low, frustrated growl. "And you're way too sweet and good for someone like me."

She arched a brow, undeterred. "How about *I* be the judge of that?" she said, then a sinful smile eased across her lips as she placed both of her hands on his chest. She stepped even closer, brazenly pressing her body right against his. "Besides, what makes you think I'm so sweet and good? Right now, I'm feeling very, very bad."

As she spoke, she lifted up on tiptoe, so when she said the last word it was against his lips, right before she kissed him. Her mouth brushed across his, her tongue flicking out to tease and taste and challenge his self-control, which didn't stand a chance against the overwhelming need battling inside him. It didn't take long for his restraint to crumble, and he reached out and slid his hands along her hips, gripping her soft curves through her jeans with his fingers as pleasure overrode everything else but the desire to take what she was offering.

Her fingers dug into his shoulders and her lips parted in another invitation, and he was the one who took the kiss deeper, exploring the recesses of her mouth with his tongue and earning a series of sexy, approving sounds that purred up from her throat and stroked along his cock like a caress. His brain short-circuited, and a harsh growl of arousal vibrated against their lips as he walked her backward until she bumped into the island. Without breaking the frantic, greedy kiss, he lifted her up and set her down on the granite surface, which was the perfect height for him to fuck her on, if he'd wanted to.

Instinctively, she widened her knees and more than a little out of his mind with wanting her, Chase didn't hesitate to step in between, right where he belonged. Grabbing her ass, he hauled her closer to the edge, aligning the ridge of his cock right up against the seam of her jeans, his mouth still devouring hers. With a sweet, needy whimper against his lips, she wrapped her legs around him and arched her body, grinding her sex against the length of dick as if there weren't any clothes separating them at all.

Framing her face in his hands as the kiss turned hotter, wilder, he thrust back, imagining what it would be like to bury every inch of his cock inside her tight, slick pussy and hear her cry out his name. To feel her clench around his shaft and come all over his dick as he pushed her over the edge and straight into a mind-bending orgasm.

The pressure and friction between them was intoxicating, as well as frustrating because it just amplified how much he wanted Lauren. Her fingers were in his hair, tugging on the strands, and even that bit of pain heightened the pleasure coursing through him. Everything about this steamy tryst was raw and unbridled, the complete opposite of bland and boring, and Jesus, he *never* did this with a woman. Obligatory foreplay was a given, yeah, but he couldn't remember the last time, if ever, he'd indulged in a lengthy make-out session that had him so close to coming in his pants.

Before he did just that and embarrassed the fuck out of himself, he pulled back, ignoring the soft sounds of disappointment she made as he ended the kiss and untangled her legs from around his waist. Her hands fell away from his hair, and they were both breathing hard as he braced his hands on the edge of the counter on either side of Lauren as he stared into her heavy-lidded eyes.

"We need to stop," he said, his voice sounding like gravel.

She shook her head, her lips red and swollen from the way he'd just ravaged her mouth. "No, we don't."

He groaned at the sultry invitation in her tone, because he was merely a man and she was temptation personified, and he clearly needed to be the voice of reason. He wasn't going to fuck her, only to end things when they returned from their weekend together, because he was not a forever kind of guy. She deserved so much better than that. *Than him.*

Settling his hands around her waist, he scooted her off the counter and set her on her feet in front of him. The beguiling way she bit her lip and looked at him said it was just a matter of time before she wore him down.

"This isn't going to happen," he said in his best, sternest tone—as much to convince her, as well as himself.

She didn't look the least bit deterred, the minx. "We'll see."

Chapter Seven

TWO WEEKS LATER, Lauren sat in the passenger seat of Chase's black Audi Coupe as they drove toward Fairview to attend her sister's wedding. Between the smooth, luxurious ride, and their casual and easy conversation as they shared superficial getting-to-know-you information about each other during the drive, the time and miles passed quickly.

Even though she and Chase had occasionally corresponded by text and talked a few times on the phone in the evenings to discuss details for the upcoming weekend, this was the first time they'd been in close proximity since the night at his place, when he'd insisted that there wouldn't be a repeat of what had happened on his kitchen counter.

Lauren meant what she'd said when she'd told Chase "We'll see". She had a few tricks up her sleeve that she hoped he wouldn't be able to resist.

With any further discussion about Chase's past clearly off the table, she'd still managed to discover interesting things about him during those chats, like him admitting that he was a history buff who was fascinated by the past Civil and World Wars and the

Vietnam conflict, and other periods in history. She was secretly happy to learn that tidbit, since her gramps served in the Vietnam War and the two men would have something to bond over.

She'd also learned that she and Chase had a lot more in common than she ever would have imagined. They both loved to watch psychological thrillers and crime shows and true-life documentaries, along with listening to classic rock music, and they also enjoyed attending cultural events in the city.

He'd told her that he'd taken Billie to the Museum Mile Festival a few months back, and while he didn't love Broadway shows because he got too antsy sitting in those small, crowded seats, he'd sucked up his discomfort because he knew how much his sister adored the whole theater experience. It was something Billie had never done until Chase had taken her to see *Wicked*, and now, according to him, she was obsessed with New York's theatrical performances.

After sharing the endearing story with Lauren, he'd laughed and told her that his sister's fixation with Broadway made gift giving for Billie very easy.

Lauren still didn't know the whole backstory between Chase and Billie, but she'd gotten the impression that he was a dedicated big brother and that he enjoyed spoiling his half-sister with all the things she'd missed out on because of her time spent in foster care. It was just another side to Chase that revealed how kind and selfless he truly was when it came to someone he cared about.

About ten miles outside of Fairview, Lauren realized there was one important thing they hadn't yet discussed, and would undoubtedly come up at some point.

"We need to agree on a story about how we met, because I know someone is going to ask," she said, glancing over to the driver's side and taking in Chase's gorgeous profile. Actually, she was shocked that her mother hadn't already posed the question, but Lauren wanted to be prepared and make sure their stories matched. "It needs to be something ordinary, because typically I'd never be orbiting in your world."

He cast a glance her way, and though he was wearing sunglasses, she could see the downward cast of his brows. "Why do you say that?"

"Let's just say that I doubt your life, and my life, would have intersected under normal circumstances," she said, trying to be polite about what she was inferring.

"I don't know," he said, absently tapping his thumb against the steering wheel. "You work at the Meridian with wealthy clients."

She shook her head and gave a small laugh. "Not quite the same, because at the end of the workday I'm a simple girl who lives in Briarwood, just outside of Queens, and you have an apartment in the Flatiron District in Manhattan. I drive an older, used Ford Taurus and you own an Audi. After paying rent, groceries, bills, etcetera, I barely have enough money left over at the end of the month to pad my savings account while I'm sure the word 'budget' isn't even a part of your vocabulary."

He was quiet for a moment before speaking. "What you *see* with me is honestly more of an expectation because of my position as a partner at the investment firm. It puts clients at ease knowing I'm entrenched in their world, but I wasn't always this wealthy," he said, confirming what she'd already suspected as he kept his focus on the two-lane road leading into her small town. "I grew up in Bay Ridge in Brooklyn. I had to pay my own way through college and racked up more debt than a young twenty-something kid should have to worry about. I ate my fair share of ramen while living in a shithole of an apartment with three other guys when I was looking for work after graduating. And just for the record, I *like* that you don't run in what is perceived as my social circles."

She stared at him in surprise, not sure what to make of that. "Why?" she asked, needing more clarification.

He glanced in her direction, and even though his eyes were shielded, she could feel the sudden intensity of his gaze. "I like that you're down-to-earth and unpretentious and *real*... because it makes it easy for me to just be myself around you."

Holy shit. The statement was so profound, so revealing of who Chase really was, that she didn't know what to say in response.

He returned his attention to the road in front of

them. "So, how about we go with something simple as far as how we met, like we were introduced by a mutual friend or acquaintance, which is partially true."

She had no idea who he was referring to. "Like whom?"

He grinned at her, and that relaxed and easy gesture made butterflies swirl in her stomach. "We both have Billie in common, and considering she really is the reason why we're in this together, let's go with that."

It made sense. She knew Billie because of the connection to Future Fast Track, and Billie was Chase's sibling. She could have easily introduced the two of them at some point. "Okay, that works."

The navigation system in Chase's car directed him to make a right at the next light, indicating that they were only minutes away from her parents' house. She'd promised her mother that she'd go to their place first so they could meet Chase and they'd stay for dinner, before they headed to their room at the bed-and-breakfast in town.

Chase cleared his throat, his fingers tightening on the steering wheel. "By the way, are your sister and Greg going to be at your parents' tonight for dinner, too?"

"No," she said, absently smoothing a hand down the skirt of the casual dress she'd worn. "My mom said that Ashley and her bridesmaids are at the wedding venue, doing some last-minute decorating for the ceremony and reception tomorrow evening." Honestly, even if that was just an excuse, Lauren was grateful and relieved, because she selfishly wanted tonight to be stress-free with Chase. Or as much as it could be, considering she knew her family would undoubtedly grill him with questions. "You'll meet them at the wedding tomorrow night."

They drove down a tree-lined street, and then they finally arrived at the house she'd grown up in, with a light blue exterior and a wraparound porch complete with a swing. Pansies, violas, and asters bloomed around the structure and a brick-inlaid walkway led up to the front steps.

As much as Lauren loved living in the city, she couldn't deny the nostalgia she experienced whenever she visited home.

Just as Chase parked the car at the curb and turned off the engine, her mother came out of the house, wearing the floral-patterned apron that Lauren had bought her for Christmas since she'd probably been preparing dinner. Her mom was followed by Lauren's dad, then Gramps, and she knew the welcome committee wasn't for her, but for the "new man in her life" they all were eager to meet.

"Looks like it's showtime," she said, glancing at Chase with a grin. "Are you ready?"

He took off his sunglasses and tucked them into the middle console, his own smile more reserved. "Ready as I'll ever be, I suppose."

❖   ❖   ❖

CHASE SECRETLY LOVED watching the enthusiastic way Lauren greeted her parents. How she ran up the walkway with abandon, hair flying out behind her and squealing in excitement as she embraced them all in a hug, while he made his way to the house at a more leisurely pace, to give her family time to welcome Lauren back home. The trio looked just as happy to see her, too, and it was hard not to envy their close-knit relationship.

As soon as he stepped up onto the porch to join them, Lauren grabbed his hand and pulled him forward, making him the center of attention as all eyes turned to him. He wasn't in the habit of formally meeting a woman's parents and he had to resist the urge to shift awkwardly on his feet, which was an anomaly for him. As a businessman in the corporate world, he was always confident and self-assured, but there was something about making a good impression on Lauren's family that had him feeling surprisingly anxious.

"Chase, meet my mom, Penny, my dad, Dale, and my gramps, Lee," she said in way of introduction. "Everyone, this is Chase Gossard."

He noticed Lauren didn't put a label on their relationship which, he was grateful for, but the way her mother's eyes lit up right before she pulled him into a quick, warm embrace told Chase that Penny had already put him into the boyfriend category. Or maybe even something more serious.

Penny didn't hug him long, and when she stepped

back she was beaming with delight. "Welcome to our home, Chase. We're so happy to finally meet you," she said, putting him completely at ease.

"Likewise," he said, thinking Penny appeared to be a more mature version of Lauren and what she'd look like when she was in her early fifties. A natural, fresh-faced beauty, with chin-length dark brown hair and sparkling brown eyes.

Chase turned to Lauren's father next, extending his hand toward the other man. Dale was stout, with broad shoulders, a solid build, and a firm handshake that conveyed mutual respect. During a conversation with Lauren, she'd mentioned that her father worked for a construction company as an electrician.

"It's nice to meet you, Mr. Connelly," Chase said, inclining his head.

The other man scoffed. "Please. No need to be formal around here. Call me Dale."

Chase glanced at the oldest man in the group, with wisps of white hair on his head, a neatly trimmed and equally white beard, and the same brown eyes that ran in the family. Except his gaze was more critical than Penny's and Dale's, as if he was trying to sum up Chase and decide if he was good enough for his granddaughter.

Smiling, Chase shook Lee's hand, his grip strong enough to convince Chase that there was nothing frail about this man who'd just suffered the equivalent of a stroke. "It's a pleasure, sir," Chase said amicably. "Lauren has told me so much about you."

Hearing that his granddaughter had mentioned him softened the older man's features. Gramps puffed his chest out, his upper body straining against the top portion of his faded, jean overalls. "All good things, I'm sure," he said, then followed that up with a feisty wink. "I *am* her favorite, after all."

Lauren laughed as she casually looped her arm through Chase's, making them look very much like a couple. "Yes, you are, Gramps."

"She mentioned you recently had a health scare," Chase said. "I hope everything is well?"

"Bah!" Lee waved a hand in the air dismissively and scowled at the reminder. "As you can see, I'm as hale and hearty as can be."

Penny rolled her eyes at Lee's dramatics then motioned toward the front door. "Come on in, you two. Dinner is almost ready."

Everyone walked inside the house and into the small, but cozy living room.

"Can I get you something to drink, Chase?" Penny asked.

He shook his head. "No, thank you. I'm fine."

"Okay, then," she said with a nod, then glanced at her daughter. "Lauren, would you mind helping me get everything on the table while the boys chat?"

"Sure, Mom."

Lauren glanced up at Chase, meeting his gaze, her own eyes silently asking if he was okay on his own so soon after meeting everyone. He gave her a subtle, reassuring nod and smiled, then she followed her mother into the kitchen. Chase took a seat on the couch, while the other men sat in the two recliners in the room.

Lee didn't waste any time interrogating him, his steely eyes slightly narrowed. "So, Scouty tells us you're a fancy-pants finance man."

Chase had to suppress a grin. He wasn't sure what amused him more. The adorable nickname Lauren's gramps had for her or the humorous job description the older man had come up with for his occupation.

"Yes, I'm a managing partner at my investment firm," he said, downplaying his title.

As proud as he was of being a partner, he didn't want to come across as a pretentious "fancy pants", as Lee had put it. These were simple people who clearly lived a modest life, and Chase wasn't above them in any way whatsoever. He also realized that he really wanted to make a good impression because shockingly, he wanted Lauren's family to like him.

"What do you do there besides play with other people's money?" Gramps asked, testing Chase once again while Dale looked on with an expression of both pity and amusement.

Chase relaxed against the sofa cushion, realizing that Lauren must have gotten her moxie from her gramps. "I do manage investment portfolios and play with other people's money, so to speak, by selling and buying securities that are a good fit for my clients," he said with a self-depreciating grin. "But I also spend a lot of time conducting research on financial markets and economic trends so I can offer my clients the best strategies for their money."

Lee asked a few more questions, and each time Chase came back with a relatable response that seemed to gain Lee's admiration and approval. When Chase felt that shift to acceptance between them, he decided to change the subject to something he knew would win the older man over for sure.

"Lauren mentioned that you served in the Vietnam War," he said, then gave the other man a nod. "Thank you for your service, sir," he added respectfully, which earned him a smile from the older man. "I'm a bit of a history buff and would love to hear about your experience."

Lee's eyes sparked with pride, and he stood up. "Come here," he said, motioning for Chase to follow him as he walked toward a glass display case in the living room. "I want to show you a few things."

Chase joined him, genuinely in awe of the *real* memorabilia in the cabinet—precious, irreplaceable awards and achievements that Lee had earned during his time in the service.

Lee pointed out all the military medals and described each one, including a Purple Heart, a Vietnam Service Medal, a Republic of Vietnam Campaign Medal, and a very rare Vietnamese Gallantry Cross. Chase was well aware of just how much emotional attachment and deep meaning these medals had to the recipient, and the dignity in Lee's voice as he spoke was unmistakable. These accolades represented hard work, tough decisions, bravery, and fearlessness during a time when the controversial war had divided the country.

While they discussed his various accolades, Lee also recounted his time in Vietnam, without going into many dark details, focusing most on the sense of brotherhood he felt with his fellow soldiers. His stories immersed Chase deep into the history that he, personally, loved so much, and he appreciated that he and Lee could share that small connection.

"Hey, you two," Lauren said from behind them, bringing Lee's storytelling to an end for now. "It's time for dinner."

Lee put all his medals back in the cabinet, and the three of them strode to the dining room, with Lauren leading the way.

Gramps slapped Chase on the back in male cama-raderie. "You know, you're not so bad, Mr. Gossard," he said in a lighthearted tone.

Chase chuckled, oddly pleased that he'd managed to secure Lee's favor.

They all sat down at the table, he and Lauren on one side, Dale and Penny across from them, and Gramps at the head. All the food was already laid out, and platters were passed around for them to serve whatever portion size they wanted.

It was such a simple thing, really, but also so family oriented. Chase couldn't remember ever sitting at a table with his parents while they were married, and after his mother left, well, he'd eaten most of his meals on a TV tray in front of the TV, or alone at the kitchen counter. There was an underlying sense of love and security in this house that he'd never had, and this caring environment brought a pang to his chest and made him truly realize everything he'd missed out on.

Penny had made beef stroganoff with noodles from scratch, along with those buttered green beans that Lauren had mentioned that night at his place as one of her favorites, and now he understood why. According to Penny, the vegetables had been picked fresh from the garden that afternoon and they'd been sauteed in butter and garlic, but their crisp, sweet flavor still came through. They were better than any side dish he'd ever had at the numerous five-star restaurants where he dined.

The discussion at the table started with Lauren giving her parents and Gramps an update on her job, and how well the Future Fast Track charity ball had gone, which had been her first big event without her boss being there. Much to Gramps's chagrin, Penny shared the details of his most recent doctor's visit so Lauren was in the loop of what was going on and how he was doing—which was *extremely well*, according to Lee.

Penny mentioned her book club, then got Lauren caught up on what Chase perceived to be town gossip. Dale was a man of few words, Chase realized. He was a listener more than a talker, which Chase could appreciate because that was him for the most part, as well.

When there was a brief lull in the conversation

near the end of the meal, Penny didn't hesitate to start asking him questions about his life in general, his family, his job, and living in New York, and yes, how he and Lauren met. All things a parent would want to know about the new man in their daughter's life.

"So, how serious are things between the two of you?" Penny asked, sliding that loaded question into the conversation. "I'm assuming pretty serious for Lauren to bring you home to meet the family."

"*Mom*," Lauren objected, sounding horrified that Penny had put him on the spot in regard to their relationship, and his intentions.

"Honey, you know your father and I have been worried about you since... well, *you know*," she said in a low voice, as if speaking in hushed tones would make the insinuation any easier to bear. "We're just happy to see you haven't sworn off men altogether and met someone so well suited to you." She beamed at Chase.

Lauren groaned, and across the table Dale just remained quiet and shook his head in resignation at his wife's meddling.

"I'm so sorry," Lauren mumbled, her face a deep shade of pink.

"Don't be." Wanting to ease her embarrassment, he impulsively reached over and grabbed her hand, bringing it to his lips and pressing a soft kiss to the back of it. Her eyes went wide at the public display of affection, and he gave her a reassuring wink before glancing back at Penny.

"Mrs. Connelly, I can appreciate you wanting the best for Lauren," he said, interjecting understanding into his tone. "And what I can tell you is that Lauren and I are still getting to know one another, but what I've discovered so far, I like. A lot," he said, realizing how true those words were, that it wasn't just perfunctory praise to appease her family. "Right now, we're taking things slow and just seeing where it goes."

"Fair enough," Dale finally chimed in, and his answer seemed to satisfy both Penny and Lee, too.

They stayed for another hour and a half, while Lauren helped her mother clean up the kitchen, then Penny served freshly made peach cobbler and coffee for dessert. It was nearing seven in the evening by the time Lauren made the excuse that they were tired after a long day and they finally said their goodbyes and left.

Chase walked Lauren to the car, opened the passenger door for her, and once she was inside, he went around to the driver's side and slid behind the wheel. As soon as both doors were shut tight and they were sealed inside, Lauren exhaled a long breath that ended on a groan.

"Thank God that's over," she said, resting her head back against the seat before glancing at him with a tired smile. "My family can be exhausting with all the talking and questions. Especially my mother and Gramps."

Without thinking, he reached over and tucked a strand of hair behind her ear so that he could see her face better in the fading twilight, and had to resist the urge to slide his hand around the back of her neck and bring her mouth to his for a slow, hot kiss. It was something he'd been dying to do since picking her up at her apartment earlier that afternoon.

"It wasn't so bad, *Scouty*," he teased, using the nickname Lee had used several times over the course of the evening.

She sighed, but the smile remained. "You were wonderful with my parents. And Gramps. You did a fantastic job winning them over and convincing them we're a happy couple with that whole spiel at the dinner table about us taking things slow and seeing where they go. I know it wasn't easy dealing with what probably felt like an interrogation at times, but thank you for being so great about everything, considering we're not in a real relationship."

Those last words were like a kick to Chase's stomach, a stark reminder that they *weren't* a couple, even though the last few hours with Lauren had been very natural, and nothing had felt forced or fake between them. As he stared into her gratitude-filled eyes, his chest tightened with the realization that a part of him wished their relationship *was* real, because he was starting to feel things for Lauren that were so much more than their fabricated romance.

It was a dangerous notion when they'd be parting ways on Sunday, probably for good. He'd promised her one weekend, and honestly, that's all he'd ever had in him to give to a woman. He didn't know the first thing about how to make a true relationship work, and he didn't trust himself not to fuck it all up with someone as vibrant and kind-hearted as Lauren.

Chapter Eight

A S LAUREN GAVE Chase the directions to the bed-and-breakfast where they'd be staying, she couldn't help but notice that he'd grown quiet and subdued since leaving her parents. There had been a noticeable shift in Chase's mood at the end of their conversation in the car before they'd driven away, and for the life of her she couldn't figure out what she might have said to cause him to revert back to the reserved man she'd met at the bachelor auction weeks ago. Not quite grumpy and standoffish, but definitely guarded once again.

The entire evening with her parents and her gramps had gone so much better than she'd anticipated. Chase had been confident, but respectful and sincere, all things that had gained favor with her father. He'd managed to charm her mother and impress her gramps, which wasn't an easy feat. In fact, on the way to the door as they were leaving, her gramps had whispered in her ear, "He's a keeper," which was probably the biggest stamp of approval Chase could have gotten from him.

But for Lauren, she couldn't forget how he'd replied to her mother's question at the dinner table, about how serious it might be between the two of them. Lauren had initially been mortified that her mother had been so bold, but the way Chase had lifted her hand to his lips for a kiss in such a sweet manner, then responded with, *"What I can tell you is that Lauren and I are still getting to know one another, but what I've discovered so far, I like. A lot,"* made everything inside of Lauren melt. In that moment, she wanted to believe those words, wanted more than anything for them to be true, but she also knew she had to be careful not to read too much into the things Chase said or did this weekend because she'd essentially hired him to be the perfect boyfriend. And that's exactly what he'd been tonight.

She glanced over to the driver's seat, seeing the slight frown on his face that made him look much too serious. Maybe Chase was just tired, she reasoned, which was something she could relate to. Between the drive and dinner at her parents', it had been a long day. And her family *was* a lot to handle if you were someone who wasn't used to so much stimuli in a short span of time.

She wanted to ask Chase if he was okay, but she refrained from doing so. The last thing she wanted was to come across as one of those women who was insecure, or needed validation when there was silence… even though she hoped Chase was in a better mood once they got to their room, since she'd made some very bold and brazen plans for their night together.

"You're going to make a left at the next stoplight, and then the Fairview Bed and Breakfast is going to be on the right," she said, giving him the last of the directions.

Minutes later, he pulled up to the curb in front of a large colonial-style house, with a gabled roof and a porch adorned with hanging baskets of flowers. A wooden sign with the name of the inn hung from an ornate wrought-iron bracket near the entrance. Lights were on inside, and a few outside, giving off a warm and inviting atmosphere.

After getting out of the car, Chase grabbed their bags from the trunk, insisting on carrying both of theirs as they walked along the cobblestone path, then up the steps to the door. The owner of the place, Betsy Martin, greeted them as they entered the inn and stepped up to the counter just off the entryway.

"Lauren, it's so good to see you!" the sixty-something woman said in a bright, cheerful tone. "Your mother mentioned that you'd be staying here the weekend of your sister's wedding, but I didn't see a reservation under your name." Her gaze shifted to Chase, sparkling with unmistakable interest as she unabashedly checked him out. "So, I'm assuming it must be under yours?"

"Yes, ma'am," he said in a polite tone, and smiled as he retrieved his ID from his wallet and passed it across the counter to Betsy to validate his reservation. "The name is Chase Gossard."

"Well, it's a pleasure to meet you, Mr. Gossard." Betsy beamed at him like a young schoolgirl, much to Lauren's amusement. "Welcome to Fairview. And Lauren, welcome home."

"Thank you," she replied, while they waited for Betsy to finish checking them in.

Warmth suffused Lauren's entire body when she felt Chase's arm drape across her shoulders and he pulled her closer to his side. Most likely just for appearances and Betsy's sake, but Lauren was not at all opposed to the intimate gesture, not to mention that his pensive mood had thawed a bit during the drive to the inn.

Betsy glanced up from her computer screen, smiling as she, too, noted how much they looked like a romantic couple. "So, your room is located on the second floor right up those stairs, at the end of the hallway. Here's your key. Breakfast is served between seven and nine in the morning in the dining area, buffet style, and you're free to enjoy the gardens out back during the day if you just need a place to sit and take advantage of this wonderful weather."

"Sounds perfect," Chase said, flashing her a charming smile.

"I hope you two enjoy your stay, and if you need anything else that's not already in your room, you just let me know."

"Will do," Lauren said, and led the way up the stairs Betsy had indicated, with Chase following behind carrying their bags.

"Well, that was nice," she said in a low voice only Chase could hear once they'd reached the second floor. "I hope the rest of the weekend goes just as smoothly."

"No reason it shouldn't with me by your side."

Reaching the last room down the hallway, she glanced over her shoulder with a cheeky grin for Chase. "Yeah, you're a great distraction. By morning, most of the town will know that I'm shacking up with a gorgeous man at the Fairview Bed and Breakfast."

He arched a brow. "Shacking up?"

She inserted the key into the knob and gave it a turn, her eyes still locked on his. "A girl can hope, right?"

Before he could reply, she opened the door and they stepped inside the spacious room, complete with a small, cozy sitting area and their own private en suite.

He set their luggage down and swore beneath his breath when he saw the single queen-size bed in the room. "I told Victoria to book *two* double beds."

That fierce frown was back again, and the last thing Lauren wanted was his assistant to get reprimanded for something that wasn't her fault. "Don't blame Victoria. She did exactly what you asked her to do. I called a few days ago and asked for one queen-size bed under your reservation."

"Why would you—" The confusion glimmering in his eyes cleared as understanding dawned. "Lauren—"

"Chase, do you want me?" she asked, interrupting what she already knew was going to be an argument she didn't want to have. She'd also decided that the direct approach was best, even though she knew there was a possibility of a rejection that would undoubtedly sting.

He groaned, his expression conflicted. "I think we've already established just how much I want you the night at my place when I nearly fucked you on my kitchen countertop."

The memory of that hot encounter caused an arousing heat to settle low in her belly. "I just wanted to make sure that hasn't changed."

"No, it hasn't," he said, bracing his hands on his hips. "But other things haven't changed, as well, like the fact that this is just one weekend together, for the sake of putting on the pretense of a happy couple. But the reality is, I don't do long term because I don't know how. I don't do commitments because I don't have that ability. I can't make you the kind of promises someone like you deserves."

She swallowed hard and let him have his say, even though the words he spoke hurt more than she'd ever admit out loud. But she'd also learned enough about Chase to know that this was his deeply ingrained belief system, that everything in his past influenced how he viewed relationships, or his ability to have one. Being alone was all he knew, and while a part of her couldn't fault him for trying to protect her, the other part, the woman who desired him, didn't want his honorable sacrifice. If this short time with Chase was all she could have of him, then she wanted it.

"I'm not asking you for a commitment, or promises," she said, and despite the nerves suddenly taking hold, she stubbornly held his gaze, her next statement just as raw and honest as his. "All I want is one no-strings-attached weekend with you, Chase. You gave me a small taste of passion that night in your kitchen, and call me greedy, but I want more. We're two consenting adults who are attracted to one another, so what is the harm in enjoying each other without the expectation of anything more? People hook up all the time."

His jaw clenched and he pursed his lips, looking torn, but he didn't say anything more and she had no idea if she'd managed to change his mind, or not.

Grabbing her suitcase, she set it on the upholstered bench at the end of the bed, then opened it up. Feeling his eyes on her, she dug through the contents until she found what she was looking for—her toiletry bag and what she planned to wear to bed.

Swallowing back the emotion gathering in her throat and schooling her features, she turned to face him again, her chin lifting. "I'm going to change and wash my face and brush my teeth, so just think about what I said… and I hope you'll change your mind by the time I come back out."

After walking into the adjoining bathroom, she closed the door then leaned back against it, exhaling a deep breath as she clutched her items to her chest, where her heart was beating so hard it echoed in her ears.

She had no idea if she'd managed to change Chase's mind, but she had one last weapon in her arsenal to try and sway him. One he hopefully wouldn't be able to resist.

✧   ✧   ✧

FEELING AS THOUGH he was about to let something incredibly special and rare slip through his fingers, Chase watched Lauren head into the en suite, head held high and shoulders straight.

That pride she displayed was nothing less than he'd expect from this woman who'd dared to challenge him more than anyone else ever had. But despite that stubborn and determined façade during her bold speech moments ago, her eyes had spoken the truth. Beneath her bravado he'd seen a vulnerability that made his heart ache and shattered all the defenses he normally had no issues keeping in place when it came to women.

The realization should have scared the shit out of him, but he was tired of fighting his attraction to Lauren when he wanted nothing more than to feel her warm, naked body beneath his and hear his name on her lips when she came all over his cock. He speared his fingers through his hair and groaned at that erotic image playing out in his head. One he'd jerked off to more than a few times since that evening in his kitchen.

She'd taken a huge risk putting herself out there the way she had, knowing he could turn her down once again. But if he was completely honest with himself, he wasn't immune to Lauren, and out of every argument she'd made there was one statement he couldn't get out of his head, no matter how hard he tried.

"You gave me a small taste of passion that night in your kitchen, and call me greedy, but I want more."

Yeah, that. So brazen and genuine and real. Like the woman herself.

If there was one thing Chase could do, it was to give Lauren what she'd asked for, what she'd never experienced with another man. And who was he kidding, anyway? The thought of any guy other than him fucking her until she was limp and sated from multiple orgasms and drunk on passion made him feel more than a little possessive.

She wanted a final answer when she came out, and he was ready to give her an honest one. Between the two of them, rules had already been established. Lauren knew where he stood, and he was prepared to agree to her no-strings-attached request. For just this weekend together, she was his, and he planned to take advantage of the next two days with her, guilt-free.

Decision made, all the tension Chase had been holding on to seemed to drain out of him and his head cleared, so he was able to relax and focus on her pleasure tonight, and nothing else.

He could hear the water running in the bathroom, and while she finished up, Chase stripped down to his boxer briefs, then sat down on the bed to wait for her to come out, his mind already jumping ahead to all the things he planned to do to her for the rest of the night.

A few minutes later the door opened, and he was unprepared for the sight that greeted him. Lauren stepped out and walked toward him, a brazen seductress in a skimpy, sheer little nightgown that had all the blood in his body rushing straight to his dick. He boldly looked his fill, taking in her small but pert breasts beneath the translucent red fabric, the curve of her waist and hips he wanted to grab with his hands, and the ridiculously tiny scrap of material posing as panties.

Lust thrummed through his veins and he raised his eyes back to hers, seeing the barest hint of nerves in the way she bit her bottom lip and shifted on her bare feet. Clearly, a part of her was bracing for a second rejection, and he quickly dispelled her misgivings by allowing a smile to lift up the corners of his mouth.

"Were you planning on wearing that to bed?" he asked, tipping his head.

She fiddled with the lacy hem of the nightie, and picking up on his playful demeanor, she responded in an equally teasing manner. "That all depends on what you've decided. I'm either going to wear it all night to torture you, or it's coming off. Your choice."

He chuckled because he loved this woman's sass. "I definitely want it off," he said, giving her the answer she'd been waiting for, and he didn't miss the relief that flickered across her features.

That was all he needed to know he'd made the right choice. *Her.*

Chapter Nine

THE ANTICIPATION AND anxiety twisting inside of Lauren vanished at Chase's agreement. She didn't ask what changed his mind and didn't care. The only thing that mattered to her was being with him and getting to experience his brand of seduction. She knew what *not* to expect from this weekend arrangement, and as long as she managed to keep her heart out of the equation, she'd be fine.

But that same heart mocked her. The deep connection she'd already formed with Chase told her she'd fallen faster than she ever could have predicted. But she couldn't bring herself to process the depth of her feelings at the moment. What she could do was focus on the immediate moment and what Chase was offering.

"So, if we're doing this, I insist on giving you the full experience," he said in a husky drawl, interrupting her thoughts and bringing her back to what they were about to do.

"And what might the full experience be?" she asked, biting her lower lip, being deliberately sexy.

"Orgasms, fucking, and dirty talk, of course," he

said, offering everything she'd dreamed of.

Her pulse quickened in anticipation as he stood up and approached her. While she'd been in the bathroom, he'd taken off everything but his underwear, and it was almost criminal that he had to wear any clothes at all because this man's body was meant to be admired *naked*. Broad shoulders. A strong, muscular chest. Firm, well-defined abs that indicated he worked out regularly. And the dark trail of hair that disappeared beneath the waistband of his tight boxer briefs that outlined the promise of a very impressive cock.

Licking her suddenly dry lips, she forced her gaze all the way back up to his, and the heat in his eyes seared her. He stood a few inches away and it was all she could do not to reach out and touch his bare skin.

Instead, she kept up their flirtation. "Tell me more about this full treatment and what it entails. I think I need specifics."

He lightly skimmed his fingers along her bare arm, and there was no mistaking the way her nipples hardened against the sheer fabric of her nightie. "It starts with me kissing your lips, then your breasts," he murmured, those same fingers tracing the low-cut neckline before drifting down her sternum. "Then continuing to your pussy and using my mouth and my tongue and my fingers to make you come… the first time."

She shivered, a small, arousing sound escaping her lips as he stroked along the front of her panties, just enough to tease before his hand fell away from her needy sex.

"I'm totally on board with that," she said breathlessly.

"And as much as I appreciate this hot little number you're wearing, it's coming off right now so I can have full access to every inch of your naked body." He brought his hands back up to her shoulders and slipped his fingers beneath the thin spaghetti straps holding up her lingerie, slowly pushing them off her arms until the material fell to the floor around her feet.

His eyes sparked with hunger as he devoured her bared breasts with his gaze, and somehow she managed an impudent grin. "It really was just to tempt you, to make you see what you were missing out on if you said no."

Arching a brow at her unabashed confession, he cupped her breasts and flicked his thumbs across her stiff nipples, making her gasp, then moan when he lightly pinched them. "I ought to spank you for being so naughty."

She loved this sexy, lighthearted side to Chase. "Mmm, I'm not opposed to that."

"Good to know." He smirked, and even that sly look on his gorgeous face made her core clench. "We'll talk about a proper punishment for you later, after the first time I fuck you. Because a spanking like that should be doled out while you're getting pounded from behind."

Her jaw dropped and her cheeks heated with a blush, because the last thing she'd expected from this normally staid man was such a filthy and unfiltered mouth in the bedroom. "Yeah, not opposed to that, either," she whispered.

He chuckled, and the dark and dirty sound slid through her veins, then down between her legs like warm honey.

He pushed a hand into her hair, gripping his fingers in the strands and taking hold so that he could tug her head back, her mouth ready for his. His lips landed on hers, and there was nothing soft or slow about the kiss. She didn't want it to be. Lust immediately erupted between them as his tongue swept inside, so deep and hungry and fierce it stole the breath from her lungs.

Dying to touch him, she pressed her palms to his chest while he continued to kiss her like she was the only thing he needed to exist. She strummed her fingers over his pecs, and then his nipples, reveling in the rumbling sound that rose up in his throat. Emboldened by that reaction, she skimmed her hand lower, until the length of his erection molded against her palm and she squeezed that rigid column of flesh she couldn't wait to feel inside her.

Within just a few strokes he tore his mouth from hers with a guttural, "Fuck," then grabbed her wrist and pulled her hand away, his features taut. "Not until I'm done with you," he said, breathing hard. "Lie down on the bed."

She eagerly obeyed the order and he joined her, pushing her legs apart so he could kneel in between. His hands grasped the sides of her flimsy panties that were already soaked with desire, and just as he started to yank them down he stopped, swearing beneath his breath as his eyes raised all the way up to hers.

"I wasn't expecting this to happen while we were here," he said, a pained look on his face. "I didn't bring any condoms."

She bit her lower lip. "I did. They're in my bag. Left-side pocket. A dozen of them." When he arched an inquisitive brow at her, she grinned and shrugged. "What can I say? I was… hopeful."

He chuckled. "And I'm grateful."

He moved off the bed, quickly and easily finding the two long strips in her suitcase. He tore off one square, and holding one of the corners between his teeth, he removed his briefs, giving Lauren her first glimpse of his hard, straining shaft. He was so thick and long, and just the thought of feeling all those inches inside her had her squirming on the mattress.

"Take off your panties for me," he said impatiently, tearing open the packet and rolling the condom down his length while she wriggled out of her underwear and tossed them aside.

And then he was back, crawling over her prone body until his face was in front of hers. Hands braced on the bed beside her shoulders and his knees bracketing her hips, he lowered his mouth to hers and kissed her again, this time a little softer, a little slower, rekindling that restless need as she threaded her fingers in his hair, clenching and unclenching them around the soft, thick strands.

The taste of him was addicting, and after another deep, decadent kiss, his lips moved on, sliding down her neck. He gently bit and sucked on patches of her skin, making her shiver and moan. He gradually moved lower, licking across her chest, beneath the curve of one breast, then the other, and when his mouth latched onto a nipple and sucked, she arched her back off the bed, silently begging him to consume her.

He did, taking more of her into his hot, wet mouth, the flick of his tongue joining in to elevate her pleasure. His teeth grazed and nipped her flesh, adding a jolt of arousing pain to the mix, and her pussy throbbed with a desperate demand for his attention, too.

As his lips scattered damp, lazy kisses along her stomach, her hands fisted tighter in his hair, eagerly and shamelessly pushing him down to where she ached and needed that mouth of his the most.

He chuckled against her belly. "Something you want, sweetheart?" he drawled, and she could hear the husky amusement in his voice when all she could do was make inarticulate sounds in the back of her throat.

But he didn't need her words. The man's sense of direction was impeccable, and it didn't take him much longer before he was settled between her spread legs, her thighs draped over his shoulders and his face so close to her sex she could feel the gust of his breath on her wet flesh.

"This," he said on a reverent groan as his hands

gripped her writhing hips to hold her in place as he swiped his tongue though her folds, making her inhale sharply. "This is what *I* want."

Then he ended the torment and feasted on her pussy, his tongue alternating between long, languid strokes, and licking and swirling around her clit. She moaned as ripples of ecstasy rolled through her, taunting her, as he kept her orgasm just out of reach. The pressure inside of her built and built and built, pushing her higher and higher, making her delirious with the need to come.

"Please, please, please," she begged, her voice filled with a desperate, wanton demand as she bucked against his mouth and tugged on his hair.

He released her hip with one hand and the next thing she knew, two thick fingers were thrusting inside her, nearly short-circuiting her brain as he fucked her with those digits and dragged the tips over a sensitive patch of skin just inside her channel, again and again.

His tongue fluttered across her clit, giving her that final push toward the orgasm she was chasing. She went wild as overwhelming sensations crashed through her, unraveling all the tension coiling tight inside her and unleashing it in a torrent of unbelievable rapture that completely engulfed her.

She cried out and shook uncontrollably, her body racked with a sublime pleasure she didn't even know existed. Her release was so powerful, so intense and overwhelming, that tears seeped from the corners of her eyes and she gasped for breath, her heart racing out of control.

Before any of those internal contractions had a chance to recede, he moved back over her, thrusting deep and catching the last pulses of her climax, the intensity in his eyes stealing her breath. He groaned, spearing one hand into her hair and using the other to hook one of her legs in the crook of his arm, spreading her indecently wide and pinning her beneath the weight of his body so that she could take every inch of him.

Angling his hips, he pumped into her fast and hard, deliberately grinding down onto her sensitive clit each time. The friction was like a spark to tinder, jolting her toward another orgasm. She gasped, her eyes widening as she stared up at him in shock.

He grunted, a knowing smirk on his face as he kept up his rapid, relentless pace. "Yeah, that's it. You feel so fucking good. Give me one more," he ground out, burying his shaft balls deep each time he slammed forward. "Do it, baby. Come for me. I want to feel your pussy squeeze around my cock."

The pleasure rushing through her was all too much, overwhelming her as she clutched his shoulders. She didn't think a second orgasm was possible, but she was wrong. Chase's dirty words, the demand in his voice, and the way he was holding back, waiting for her to tip over first, combined to make her combust all over again. Her lips parted, and as if he knew she was about to scream, he placed a hand over her mouth to muffle the sound so she didn't bring Betsy, or any other guests in nearby rooms, running.

As another tidal wave of sensation racked her body, he grunted, and she watched as his restraint finally snapped, his jaw clenched tight. With one final thrust, he stiffened above her, his chest heaving and his eyes rolling back as he groaned through his own release, his hips jerking hard against hers until he was completely spent.

She reveled in the moment, in him, and the on-slaught of emotions coursing through her—contentment, adoration, and unbridled passion. He'd given her exactly what she'd wanted, and so much more.

After he recovered, he stood to take care of the condom before settling in beside her. Turning to face her while she lay on her back, he placed a hand on her stomach, skimming his fingertips over her skin as a lazy, mellow smile touched his lips. "You, Lauren Connelly, are going to be the death of me."

"Not so quick," she teased, shaking her head and basking in the warmth of his surprisingly tender gaze on her face. "We still have eleven condoms left to use."

He laughed, the sound loose and easy and relaxed, and one she loved hearing from Chase. "Not sure I'm going to survive the weekend with you, but what a way to go."

Chapter Ten

C HASE SLOWLY AWOKE to a warm, soft backside wriggling against his groin, making his morning erection even stiffer, painfully so, as his dick lodged itself against a bare, curvy ass.

Certain he was in the throes of some kind of dream, he gradually peeled his eyes open, and it took him a moment to remember where he was, and who he was with. Not that he could ever forget Lauren Connelly, but this situation was a novelty for him. Spending the night, *an entire night*, with a woman. And waking up with her in a bed. He'd always been careful to take any female to a nice hotel for a hookup, or if they went to someone's place it was always hers. Both scenarios made it easy for him to be gone before morning so there was no misconstruing that their one-night stand was anything more than that.

The circumstances with Lauren were completely different, considering their fake relationship pact and sharing a room together for the weekend. Leaving her in the middle of the night hadn't been an option, and while the situation was new to him, he couldn't deny that he liked waking up with *this* woman in his bed.

Shockingly, he wasn't even opposed to the fact that they were essentially *cuddling*, when normally he avoided that kind of intimacy.

Nestled up to one another certainly wasn't how they'd initially dozed off. Last night, after a very robust round two, and a third shortly after that, they'd finally fallen asleep on their own sides of the bed, with plenty of space between them. He'd always been a side sleeper, but clearly, during the night, she'd scooted toward him so that her naked backside was spooned against his chest, stomach, and thighs. And at some point, he'd unconsciously draped an arm around her waist as if it were the most natural thing in the world to do.

As he laid there, secretly enjoying the feel of Lauren in his arms, she moved her hips again, swiveling them back against his rock-hard dick. Slowly, sinuously. Enough to let him know that she was awake, too, and deliberately arching and undulating that bare, tempting bottom of hers to get a reaction out of him.

He tightened his arm around her waist. "Stop squirming," he growled against her shoulder.

"I can't help it," she said in a husky whisper that was filled with mischief as she continued to wreak havoc with his self-control. "Something hard is poking me in the back."

An abrupt gust of laugher escaped him at her cheeky comment. "That's what happens when you keep wriggling your sweet little ass against my dick. It gets hard and *pokes*. Now be still or I'm going to have to take a cold shower."

"Why?" Her hand reached around, finding his cock and stroking his length, her palm soft and her fingers firm around his shaft. "It would be a shame to let this go to waste."

He groaned, and she released his dick and rolled onto her stomach beside him, then turned her head and looked at him, her hair a sexy, tousled mess around her beautiful face. She tugged on her bottom lip with her teeth, hesitating only a moment before saying, "I *really* liked it when you fucked me from behind last night."

Yeah, she had. That memory would be emblazoned in his mind, of how he'd put a nice pink palm print on her ass while she'd shamelessly pushed back against him so he'd take her harder, deeper. That position had driven her wild, and she'd had to bury her face in the pillow to muffle the sounds she'd made when she'd climaxed.

Unable to resist this woman and what she wanted, Chase grabbed another condom and that's how they started their day, with a slow, lazy, unhurried morning fuck and mutual orgasms, following by a long, hot shower together. Then, breakfast down in the dining room, where they ate an array of freshly cooked dishes and chatted with another couple who were staying at the inn while visiting friends who lived in Fairview. They weren't anyone that Lauren already knew, but she was so friendly, and he loved watching how easily she engaged in conversation while he enjoyed a second cup of coffee.

Once the couple left the dining table and it was just the two of them, and they were finished with breakfast, she turned toward him.

"So, we've got most of the day to ourselves," she said, putting her napkin on her empty plate. "How about I show you the main part of town?"

He tipped his head and absently tapped his fingers on the table. "You don't have any wedding-related things you need to do or help with?"

She shook her head, and though she smiled as if it didn't matter, there was no missing the quick flicker of sadness in her eyes before it was gone. "I'm not part of the bridal party, so I'm off the hook."

"I'm sorry," he said, meaning it. "As Ashley's sister, you should be."

She shrugged. "Too awkward, and it's fine," she insisted, brushing it off, though he could tell not being included hurt despite her bravado. "All you and I need to do is show up later this afternoon for the wedding ceremony and reception. And since we have the next few hours free, we can stroll around Fairview's equivalent of Main Street and relax and just enjoy the day. It's not far from here, so we can walk."

"Okay," he said, genuinely curious to know more about this small town where Lauren was born and raised.

They left the bed-and-breakfast, and side by side they walked leisurely along the sidewalk that led into the heart of Fairview. Their hands brushed once, then twice, just because of their close proximity, and when it happened a third time Chase slipped his hand into hers and took hold of it.

She blinked up at him in surprise, even as she curled her fingers around his. "Look at you, being the attentive, demonstrative boyfriend," she teased with a smile. "You almost make it hard to remember the grumpy guy I bought at the bachelor auction."

He inwardly winced at the reminder of how gruff and difficult he'd been with her that first night, which somehow seemed like a lifetime ago. When he was with Lauren, he didn't feel like that same cantankerous, standoffish man. How could he be when she was always so upbeat and optimistic?

He didn't want to make a quip about holding her hand for appearances' sake and minimize the truth of how he felt about her in that moment. "I like holding your hand."

She laughed lightly and ducked her head so he couldn't see her face. "You shouldn't say things like that, or else you're going to make me fall for you, for real."

Her tone was teasing, but there was a little voice in the back of Chase's head that reminded him he still needed to be careful with Lauren and her emotions. That at the end of this weekend, they'd both go back to their separate lives. The last thing he wanted to do was lead her on, or give her false hope, because there was one thing he knew about himself, and that was his inability to be the kind of fully committed man Lauren was worthy of. A man who could give *all* of himself to her.

He didn't know shit about love, not when he'd seen and lived the worst of it.

As they reached the small but bustling center of town, Chase shoved those thoughts from his mind as Lauren started regaling him with all the different connections she had to the various landmarks. From the hardware store where she had her first job as a cashier to the bowling alley and small theater where all the teens hung out on the weekends because there wasn't much else to do.

Over the next few hours, they meandered through her favorite antique shop and perused the used bookstore, where he found and purchased a few history books on the Civil War to add to his collection at home. As they made their way down the main street and browsed other specialty boutiques, Lauren introduced him to people she knew that stopped her to say hello. A few mentioned Ashley's wedding that evening, and there were a lot of speculative glances cast their way from across the streets, all of which made him feel protective of Lauren and strangely possessive, but for the most part everyone they spoke with was very welcoming and kind.

Chase couldn't remember the last time he'd felt so relaxed and stress-free. Being away from his high-powered job and the fast pace of New York City and his life there, this town was a whole different world. And he genuinely loved that he didn't know anyone.

There were no expectations of him, and there was no need to impress anyone. It was an incredibly freeing feeling, one that made him feel peaceful and content, even if he knew it was only temporary.

Still hand in hand, they continued toward a large marble fountain that was surrounded by a lush green park with families and children enjoying the beautiful day. Before they could cross the street to head in that direction, Lauren came to an abrupt stop in front of what appeared to be a clothing boutique and let out a soft little gasp when she looked at the mannequin in the window display.

The fiberglass model was wearing a long gown in a lavender hue, with a slit up one leg and a fitted bodice. The shoulder straps were accented with crystals that matched the ones defining the waistline of the dress. It was a simple, but very elegant gown.

"Oh, wow," she breathed in awe, her eyes wide. "Marie is such an amazing seamstress and always makes the most stunning dresses. This one is just beautiful and lavender is my favorite color." She turned her head and smiled impishly. "It's silly, but when I was a little girl I'd always walk by her store and imagine wearing her dresses one day."

"Why don't we go inside and you can try it on?" he suggested.

She immediately shook her head. "It's much too fancy."

"We're going to a wedding tonight," he pointed out with a grin. "That's the best place to wear something special and fancy."

She laughed and shook her head once again, trying to minimize her initial interest and the wistful look he'd seen in her eyes. "A new gown isn't in my budget. I have a dress that will be just fine for tonight." She started to walk away from the boutique, tugging him along. "Come on. I want to show you something I think you'll appreciate."

They crossed the street to the community park, and she led the way to the marble fountain. At the top was a bronze statue of a saluting soldier sitting atop a horse from the Civil War, the Union side. There were plaques all along the circular base of the fountain, embedded into the marble. He immediately noticed the name Connelly engraved into the metal a few times, along with dates that matched when the war was fought.

"This is my great-great-grandfather and two uncles on my dad's side of the family," she said, running the pad of her finger across the names before moving on to the name Patterson and pointing them out, too. "And this man right here was my gramps's great-grandfather, and his uncle, too, who all served in the Union Army."

Her family was more ingrained in this small town than Chase realized. "That's a lot of generations living in Fairview."

She nodded and smiled up at him. "The Connellys were part of a group of settlers who founded the town, and have lived here for six generations."

A light breeze blew, and he raised his free hand and brushed a strand of hair off her cheek, just as an excuse to touch her. "Looks like you broke tradition by moving to New York."

She shrugged. "I probably would have lived my entire life here and raised my own family in this town... had I married Greg," she said, but there wasn't an ounce of regret in her tone. "It's a lovely community, for sure, but I've never had any doubts about moving to the city. It's where I belong."

Now that he knew Lauren, he could easily agree. She was much too vivacious to be confined to a stereotypical small town box for the rest of her life. Obviously, she still loved Fairview because it's where her roots were, and where the rest of her family resided, but he understood how someone like her thrived in New York City.

A distinctive melody filled the air, and Lauren glanced past him and grinned. "Pete's here!" she announced, and he followed the direction of her gaze to see an older man pushing what looked to be a food cart of some sort. "How about an ice cream?" she asked. "Pete makes his own and it's so good."

Seeing the excitement sparkling in her eyes, as if this was something she'd enjoyed many times growing up, he couldn't deny her request. Not that he could refuse this woman much of anything, Chase realized.

"Sure," he agreed, and let her pull him over to where the older man had parked the cart, that tinkling music still trilling in the air and drawing families to the treat.

They stepped in line and when it was their turn, Pete's eyes went wide when he saw who was standing in front of him.

"Lauren!" he exclaimed in a fond tone. "How have you been? How's the big city life in New York treating you?"

"Just great, Pete," she said, her typical infectious grin lighting up her face. "It's nice to see you're still peddling the best ice cream in the state."

He scoffed at the compliment, but he was smiling as his gaze shifted to Chase, who was still holding her hand. "And who is this young man with you? He doesn't look like a local."

"He's not." Lauren beamed up at him before returning her gaze to Pete. "This is Chase. He's here with me for the weekend, to attend my sister's wedding."

"Ahhh," Pete said with an understanding nod. "Well, welcome back. What can I get for the two of you?"

He opened the lid on the top of the cart, revealing tubs of various ice cream flavors inside the freezer compartment. Chase opted for a single serving of freshly churned butter brickle on a regular cone, while Lauren selected two scoops, one strawberry and the other chocolate.

They found a vacant park bench and sat down to eat their dessert, which admittedly the most delicious ice cream Chase ever had. He finished his cone first, and since he found watching Lauren's tongue slowly lick around her ice cream too damned erotic, he diverted his attention and pulled out the books he'd bought earlier on the Civil War. He skimmed through the pages, immersing himself in the pictures and explanation of each captured moment of battle.

"Sooo," Lauren started tentatively, prompting Chase to glance up at her to see why she sounded so hesitant, and realized she'd finished her own ice cream cone at some point. "Is a love of history something you shared with your father?" she finally asked.

The question made him visibly tense, as any discussion about his father did, and even though she'd clearly seen him stiffen at her inquisition, she didn't try to backtrack or recant her question, even knowing what a landmine she was possibly walking into. Instead, her unflinching gaze held his, so hopeful and compassionate, even.

She was giving him an opening to share something deeply personal with her, and he couldn't forget the last time she'd made a casual comment about his dad and how he'd snapped at her, that anger and resentment he harbored toward his parent always simmering beneath the surface. Talking about Eli Gossard in any capacity had always been like picking off a scab on an old wound, but as he stared into Lauren's caring eyes, he realized that he desperately wanted those scars to heal. He didn't know if it was even possible, but this time, he didn't try to evade, or avoid, the painful conversation.

"No," he finally said in a quiet tone. "Getting lost in history books was my escape and distraction from the life I was *living* with my father."

Her eyes were brimming with questions, but she remained silent, allowing him to make the decision of whether or not he continued to give her a glimpse into his own childhood and past. Knowing there would be no judgement from Lauren, he allowed those walls to lower enough to give her a glimpse into his past.

Setting aside the history books next to him on the bench, he exhaled a deep breath and dove in before he lost the nerve, starting at the beginning so Lauren could understand the whole story. "My parents, Eli and Darlene, got married because they were pregnant with me. I doubt love ever played into that decision, because from as young as I can remember, they fought constantly. Loud, bitter, nasty fights that were horrific to watch, and hear, as a kid. The things they said to one another were so awful and hurtful. The one thing my mother would always tell my father was that she never would have married him if she hadn't gotten knocked up with me, which of course, made me feel as though *I* was the issue."

"I'm so sorry, Chase," she said softly, and he didn't miss the ache in her voice.

He leaned forward, bracing his forearms on his knees, and stared down at the concrete beneath his leather loafers, determined to finish the story. "When I was seven, one day I came home from school and my mom was gone. She'd left my father for another guy, and my father told me they were getting a divorce." He cast a glance at Lauren, his own heart twisting in his chest at the pain he saw in her eyes, *for him*. "She never said goodbye to me. She just packed up her things and left, and I never saw or spoke to her again, so I thought her leaving was all my fault. That I was to blame."

She scooted closer on the bench, until she was right next to his side, then looped her arm through his and gave it a gentle squeeze. "You were just a kid, Chase."

He nodded, surprised by just how good her comfort felt when he was so used to suppressing his emotions. "I know, but that's what seven-year-olds do. They internalize everything, and I was really good about burying all my anger and pain and that sense of abandonment I felt not just from my mother, but my father, too."

"How so?" she asked quietly.

He scrubbed a hand along his clenched jaw, forcing himself to relax, which wasn't easy when those old memories reminded him of how bad and emotionally damaging things had been. "You'd think my father would see a divorce as a way to start out fresh and new, but instead he fell into a deep, dark depression, to the point that everything in his life fell apart because he couldn't stop feeling sorry for himself. He started drinking, and ignored me for the most part. He lost his job and after unemployment ran out, instead of looking for a new job he went on welfare and did nothing but stay home, drink, and watch TV. How fucking lazy and irresponsible is that?" He couldn't hold back the bitterness that seeped into his voice.

"I can't imagine how difficult that had to be for you," she said empathetically.

He huffed out a humorless laugh. "Yeah, since my father was basically useless, I grew up pretty damn quick, starting at the age of seven. If I wanted to eat, I had to scrounge through the cupboards for food and make my own meals, and his, too, or else he'd just drink beer for dinner. If I needed new clothes, I had to beg my father for a few dollars so I could buy pants and T-shirts and shoes at Goodwill. I did the laundry and the cleaning and made sure I was up in the morning for school, because my father was usually passed out from the night before. And when I was old enough, I took on a paper route and mowed neighbors' lawns to make extra money to pay for household things."

"So, you took care of your father, and got nothing in return."

"Yeah, pretty much. I was the parent from the age of seven until I left for college at eighteen." He leaned back against the bench, and as he watched all the families enjoying the beautiful fall day with their kids at the park, he felt a pang of envy for what he'd missed out on. "The thing is, I wouldn't have cared about any of that if my father had just tried to be a better person who didn't wallow in self-pity."

Lauren cleared her throat and paused for a moment before speaking, as if unsure how he'd react to her next comment. But true to her dauntless personality, it didn't stop her from bringing up another painful topic. "Billie didn't give me details, but she did mention that you didn't even know about her until a few years ago, when your father was dying."

"Yeah, that was a shocking little surprise my dad sprang on me a few days before he passed away of kidney failure," he said, his tone gruff. "When my mother left us, my father knew she was pregnant with another man's kid, and for some reason he wanted to clear his conscience before he died by letting me know I had a half-sibling. So, when he was gone, I hired an investigator to track down my mother and get me whatever details he could on my half-sibling. I honestly didn't know what I was going to do with the information. I was mostly pissed at the entire situation and never really thought I'd ever contact my mother or my brother or sister... until I read the investigative report and found out what happened to Billie."

He pressed his lips into a grim line, remembering how horrified he'd been to learn what his sister had been through. "My mother is just another shining example of a self-centered, inadequate parent. Not just for abandoning me, but for staying with an asshole of a man who had a drug addiction and who would give up his own child to the system after Darlene died because he didn't want to raise a child he didn't want in the first place. Billie was only eight at the time and spent the rest of her childhood in foster care."

Lauren gasped in shock, clearly not aware of those appalling details. "How could a parent do that to their child?"

Deeply rooted anger twisted inside him. "I honestly don't know, but I made contact immediately with Billie, even though I knew she was doing well on her own, considering how she'd grown up. But despite everything, she's my sister, someone who also was a victim of circumstances beyond her control, because of the shitty decisions and choices our mother made. I…" His voice cracked unexpectedly, and he swallowed back the sudden tightness in his throat. "I wanted Billie to know that she wasn't alone in the world, because I knew what that loneliness felt like. That I cared about her and wanted to give her the kind of stability she grew up without. I wanted to be someone she could depend on, always."

Lauren looked up at him, her soulful eyes on his face as she slid her palm down his arm, until her hand clasped his and her fingers held on tight. "You're such a good man, Chase."

His laugh was self-depreciating, because he didn't always feel like what constituted a decent man. "I think we've already established that I'm no white knight."

"I disagree." She lifted up and placed a soft kiss on his cheek. "You are for Billie, and that's all that matters."

They grew quiet as she rested her head on his

shoulder, still cuddled up to his side as they sat on the park bench together. He stroked his thumb along the back of the hand still secure in his, appreciating the peaceful moment with Lauren. A light breeze blew, gently ruffling her hair, and the sights and sounds of everything around them came back into focus. The chirping birds, the faint musical jingle of Pete's ice cream cart, the laughter and happy young voices of the children playing on the nearby swing set and jungle gym.

Everything happening around them seemed so light and carefree, and he let it all sink in, feeling unexpectedly content—something he never would have thought possible after discussing his painful past. He'd anticipated being angrier, more bitter after reliving those traumatic events. But Lauren's calm and caring acceptance seeped into his bones, soothing those frayed edges of his emotions, and he was so grateful for her compassion.

The vibration of Lauren's cellphone in her jeans pocket burst their little bubble of tranquility, much to his disappointment. She retrieved the device and swiped it open, reading whatever message had come through.

He felt her stiffen beside him. "Oh, wow," she murmured.

His first thought went to her gramps, hoping the old man was fine. "Everything okay?"

She straightened from where she'd been snuggled up to his side, and he immediately missed the connection between them. "I... I don't know," she said, a frown furrowing her brow. "I just got a text from Ashley. She asked if she could meet me at the inn to talk before she has to get ready for the wedding."

"What does that mean?" he asked, very aware of the anxious look on her face, and the way she chewed her bottom lip.

She exhaled a deep breath as she sent her sister an "OK" text back. "I have no idea, but I guess I'm going to find out."

Chapter Eleven

THE WALK BACK to the inn was quiet as Lauren tried to anticipate what her sister wanted to discuss with her after so many years of silence and awkward family get-togethers. She had no idea what to expect, but since Ashley had made the attempt to reach out on a day as important as her wedding day, then Lauren knew whatever the conversation, it had to be something very significant.

Or at least she hoped it would be.

But for right now, she kept her focus on Chase, who'd opened up and allowed himself to be vulnerable with her as he shared details of his past, his childhood, and what it meant to him to find Billie. She'd heard the pain in his voice as he spoke, had felt the depth of heartache this proud, normally closed-off man kept so well protected behind a fortress made of steel.

He'd lowered those gates for her, releasing the burden he'd been carrying for years. He let her see the pain that had been the catalyst for keeping everyone but Billie at arm's length. The fact that he had so much affection for his sister gave Lauren hope that he'd possibly make room in his life for someone else, too.

Whether or not that person was her, she didn't know. But despite what happened between her and Chase after this weekend, she wanted him to be happy, and to know that he deserved to be loved just as much as anyone else did, despite the dreadful role models he'd had in his life.

Now that they'd reached the inn, they had to part ways for Lauren to meet with her sister, which was the last thing she wanted after their profound moment together at the park. And knowing what time alone could do, possibly make him overthink things and shut her out again, she searched for a way to reassure him that all his secrets were safe with her. And she was humbled by the fact that he'd shared them with her.

Reaching the pathway that led up to the establishment where they were staying, she stopped before they could go inside and turned to face him. His eyes were clear as they met hers, his expression composed but relaxed. There was no trace of the resentment and bitterness he'd displayed earlier while discussing his parents.

She reached for and held both of his hands in hers. "Thank you for sharing everything with me today. You didn't have to, and I know it was difficult, but I appreciate you trusting me with something so difficult and painful to relive."

"It felt good to get it out," he admitted, the smile on his lips making her heart lift optimistically. "It doesn't change anything that happened, I know, but it made me realize just how long I've kept everything bottled up inside."

That he'd come to that realization on his own was huge, Lauren knew. But she was also aware that time alone, after they parted ways right now, could bring back intrusive thoughts. She had more to say, and instead of waiting until later, she said them now before this intimate moment between them was gone.

"I care about you, Chase," she said, knowing she was putting her emotions on the line, but she wasn't one to skirt the truth, even at the risk that he didn't reciprocate those feelings. "What happened to you… it shouldn't define the rest of your life, or your chance at happiness. I believe that everyone has choices to make in their lives. That there are crossroads you come to where you can elect to stay on the path you've been traveling your entire life and *wish* things were different, or you can rise above whatever tragedy you've endured and completely alter the direction of your future, for the better, and be able to look back on that choice without any regrets."

He stared at her for a long moment, his eyes searching hers as if he'd find some kind of magical answer for himself there. Then, he canted his head and spoke. "Is that what you did when you found out about your sister and Greg?"

She remembered vividly the two choices she'd been faced with. Let animosity and hatred burn in her heart, or embrace forgiveness, even if that had been extremely difficult to do at the time. She'd chosen the latter, which had enabled her to eventually be happy with her life, even though she'd ended up alone.

"I had to let it go," she said, wanting him to understand her healing process. "Don't get me wrong. It was hurtful and painful and it would be so easy to be bitter or spiteful over their deceit, but what good would that do me? If I carried around all that anger, it would never allow me to be happy with someone else."

He was quiet, a pensive look in his eyes, and Lauren hoped that her words soaked in, that they gave him the strength to make better, more forgiving choices of his own going forward. Selfishly, because she wished they could move forward together, but she also knew that was a lot to expect from a man who'd lived his life so guarded and pessimistic about relationships. She was smart enough to know that one pseudo therapy session wasn't going to magically transform a mindset that had been conditioned to believe the worst of people for the majority of his life.

"You go ahead and talk to your sister," he finally said, jutting his chin toward the front door to the inn. "I'm going to take a walk instead of sitting in the room. I've got a lot to process."

"Okay." She released his hands, hating to let him go when he was so contemplative like this. But she'd done her part, said her piece, and the rest was up to him to apply, or not. "I'll text you when I'm finished with Ashley."

He nodded and gave her a warm smile. "Good luck."

"Thanks."

They went their separate ways, and Lauren walked into the bed-and-breakfast, preparing herself to face her sister, with no buffers between them. Usually her parents and Gramps were around whenever she'd been in the same room as Ashley since the incident, and they'd awkwardly kept their distance after equally uncomfortable "hellos".

Betsy was at the counter just off the entryway, and smiled brightly when she saw Lauren. "Your sister stopped by and is out in the garden waiting for you."

She saw the curiosity in the other woman's eyes. People in town knew of their strained relationship—though not the truth about what really happened between her, Greg, and her sister—and she was just glad that they didn't comment on it, because it really wasn't any of their business.

Exhaling a deep, fortifying breath to face whatever lay ahead, Lauren walked through the back door that led to the inn's backyard, which was beautifully landscaped with an expansive green lawn, a few different sitting areas and firepit, and an array of seasonal flowers in bloom. A cobblestone pathway led to a white, ornate gazebo, and that's where Lauren saw her sister, standing beneath the shaded structure.

Lauren walked in that direction and climbed the stairs, noting the way her sister nervously twisted her fingers together and the anxiety in her pretty blue eyes. She also noticed how stunning her sister looked, how her beautiful blonde hair had been curled and secured in an elaborate updo with crystal hair pins, and her makeup was flawless, as if she'd already started the process of getting ready. The only thing Ashley seemed to be missing was her wedding gown.

Ashley didn't step forward to initiate a hug or any physical contact, and neither did Lauren. But she did tip her head and smile at her sister, trying to ease the tension in the air between them.

"Shouldn't you be at the church preparing for your pre-wedding photos?" she asked in a light tone. "The ceremony is only a few hours away."

"Yes, but coming here to speak with you was more important."

Those words spoke volumes, and wanting to hear what her sister had to say, Lauren indicated toward the wooden bench running along the interior of the gazebo. "Why don't we sit down?"

Ashley nodded jerkily as Lauren took a seat, then her sister did, too, a good three feet away. She continued to wring the hands that were now in her lap, her gaze bouncing everywhere before landing on Lauren's face. A full awkward minute of silence stretched between them, but Lauren refused to speak first or make small talk, since she wasn't the one who'd requested this impromptu meeting.

Her sister swallowed hard before finally speaking. "I don't even know where to begin, except to say I'm sorry."

Lauren realized that this apology could encompass many things that had happened between them during their lifetime, and even knowing she wasn't making things easy on her sister—and really, why should she?—she asked in a nice, but blunt way, "What, exactly, are you sorry for, Ashley?"

"So many things," she whispered, contrition in her tone as she bowed her head, before glancing up again. "Mostly, for the way things happened between Greg and I, and the way you found out about us."

Lauren figured that confession was a start, but she remained quiet, giving her sister the time and space to continue without interruption. She wasn't about to fill the silence with platitudes, or tell Ashley it was okay when Lauren deserved an explanation, and yes, even remorse.

"What we did, what *I* did, was wrong. I know that," she said, a believable ache of regret in her voice. "And there is no excuse for the way we handled our attraction and affair, or the fact that we were seeing one another behind your back. Greg should have ended things with you before the two of us started up anything."

Lauren opened her mouth to agree, but Ashley jumped up from her seat and started pacing the small area inside the gazebo, clearly not done talking and getting things off her chest.

"I know it's hard to believe, but I didn't do it to hurt you. And neither did Greg," she said, glancing at Lauren while walking back and forth. "If I'm being completely honest, I had a crush on Greg while the two of you were dating, and when I started working at the vet's office, I admittedly began flirting with him. I'm... I'm the one who initiated our first kiss, and things just snowballed and intensified from there."

Surprise rippled through Lauren. She'd always imagined that Greg had pursued Ashley, so learning the truth was... a shock.

"Greg intended to break things off with you," Ashley continued in a rush of breath, as if she needed to get everything out in the open. "He told me he felt so guilty, and honestly, I did, too, because... at that point my infatuation with him had developed into love. Unfortunately, you caught us before we did the right thing. That doesn't negate the fact that we had an affair behind your back, and I'm really, really sorry it happened."

Lauren's mind whirled as she tried to process everything Ashley just revealed. "Why didn't you just tell me all this, and the truth, when it happened? Instead of letting everything fester between us for the past two years?"

"Because... I felt incredibly guilty," Ashley replied, and tears of genuine regret shimmered in her eyes. "I did everything wrong, and I didn't know how to handle things or fix it. And the longer time went by, the harder it was to reach out and have the discussion."

"So, why now?" Lauren asked, needing to know.

Ashley bit her bottom lip before responding. "Because I need to know that you forgive me, and that you're okay with me marrying Greg. I know that's a lot to ask, and it's probably incredibly selfish of me to want your approval, but you're my sister and I do love you and I *never* intended to deliberately hurt you. You're my only sibling and you should have been a part of my wedding and I royally screwed it all up!"

Without thinking, out of pure emotional instinct, Lauren popped up from her seat and closed the distance between her and Ashley. For the first time in years, she hugged her sister, and Ashley embraced her back, holding her tight.

"Of course I forgive you," she whispered.

"Thank you," Ashley said, and as they drew apart a tear escaped the corner of her eye.

She quickly pulled a tissue from the pocket in the dress she wore and dabbed at the moisture before any more could fall and ruin her makeup. "Crap," she said on a sniffly laugh. "I knew this was going to happen."

Lauren chuckled, too, before turning serious once again. "Everyone makes mistakes. None of us are perfect, and all I truly want is for you to be happy," she said, and meant it. "And if Greg is the one who makes that happen, then that's all that matters."

"He does," Ashley said, and the way her eyes lit up told Lauren just how much her sister did love Greg. "He really, really does."

Ashley gently wiped at her nose so she didn't smear her foundation, a small frown pulling between her perfectly plucked brows as she met Lauren's gaze. "There's… more, since I'm being honest with you," she said, her tone a bit hesitant.

Lauren wasn't expecting *more* in terms of another confession from Ashley, and she braced herself for whatever was about to come next. "Okay."

"Growing up… I know we were never close, and that was my fault, too," she began, a pained look in her eyes. "I've never told anyone this before, but I was always so jealous of you."

Lauren felt her jaw drop open, and had to snap it shut as she digested her sister's unexpected, and startling, announcement. "Jealous of me? Why?"

Ashley winced in embarrassment. "Because everything came so easily to you. Fishing and riding horses and playing softball, and anything else you did. You were so talented and smart and self-assured. I'd hear that from the kids in school and the people in town when they talked about you. In comparison, I was uncoordinated and awkward and just… pretty."

Lauren's eyes widened and she covered her mouth but was unable to catch the burst of laughter before it escaped her.

"What's so funny?" her sister asked, almost indignantly.

Lowering her hand back down to her side, she gave her sister a compassionate smile. "Ashley… *pretty* is not a bad thing to be. There were times, growing up, that I envied how pretty you were, and hated how much of a tomboy I was."

It was Ashley's turned to look shocked. "Why? Your beauty is understated. And you're so confident," she said, complimenting Lauren in a way she never

147

had before. "You've never cared about other people's opinions. And I cared too much about what people thought of me. So, since I couldn't do those things that you excelled at, when a friend's mother said I should be in beauty pageants, that's what I did. I wanted to show you and Mom and Dad that I was good at something, too, even if it was something that was superficial and frivolous."

Oh, wow. Lauren stared at her sister, seeing her in a whole different light. Finally seeing all the insecurities and vulnerabilities Ashley had lived with, that Lauren never knew existed.

Reaching out, she grabbed Ashley's hands and gave them an affectionate squeeze. "I think we just need to accept and love each other for who we are. No expectations. No comparisons."

Ashley nodded, and smiled, her expression filled with relief. "I agree. See, you're so smart."

Lauren shrugged, then grinned. "Sometimes I am," she said, lightening the moment.

A jingling sound rent the air, and Ashley reached into the same pocket as she'd gotten a tissue from earlier and withdrew her cellphone. She checked the text message and a flash of panic passed over her features.

"That's Maggie, my bridesmaid," she said, her eyes wide. "I didn't mean to be here so long and she's letting me know that the photographers will be at the church in half an hour. I need to go so I can finish getting ready."

"Yes, you do," Lauren agreed. "Come on, I'll walk you out front."

They headed out of the gazebo and followed another pathway to a side gate that led around the house, instead of going through the inn. When they reached the street, Ashley stopped beside a light blue sedan parked by the curb.

"Thank you," her sister said again, the words and her tone heartfelt. "For forgiving me for how stupid and selfish I was, and for hurting you. Having you in my life is so important to me because not only do I want my sister back, but someday I'm going to have kids and they are going to need their aunt to spoil them rotten."

Lauren grinned, loving the idea of being an aunt, *and* being a part of Ashley's life again. "You can count on that."

Ashley took a step toward her car, then stopped, casting Lauren a curious look. "So, Mom said the date you brought for the weekend, Chase, is a very nice man."

Lauren nodded. "He is."

Her sister's gaze searched Lauren's face. "Are you... happy?"

She knew Ashley was insinuating her being happy with Chase, which made Ashley's question difficult to answer. In this moment, this weekend, she was very hopeful when it came to Chase, but there was no telling what the future would bring, if anything.

So, she replied with a more generic, and truthful,

version. "I'm happy with my life, yes."

"I'm so glad," Ashley said softly, genuinely. "You deserve to find someone special."

As her sister got into her car and drove away, Lauren had the thought that she wanted that with Chase. So much. But whatever happened after this weekend was ultimately up to him, and she wasn't sure that he was ready or willing to take a leap of faith with her.

But at least they had this one last night together, and she intended to make the most of it. To show Chase just how good they could be together, if he'd just open himself up to the possibility.

The rest would be up to him.

Chapter Twelve

FEELING MUCH MORE optimistic about her relationship with Ashley, Lauren walked back into the inn through the front door after seeing her sister off. She'd checked her cell and had received a text from Chase that he'd returned from his walk, and found him sitting at the dining room table with Betsy, drinking an iced tea and eating one of the homemade chocolate chip cookies set on a plate in front of him.

Surprise lit up his eyes when he saw her. "Where did you come from?" he asked, his tone light and relaxed. "I thought you were in the garden out back."

"I was," she said, taking a seat in the chair next to his. "I walked Ashley out front from the backyard's side gate, so it was easier to come in the front door. What are you two up to?" She glanced from Chase to Betsy sitting across the table, hoping that the older woman was behaving herself.

Betsy beamed at her. "I was just regaling Chase with stories of your acting debut in high school as Wendy Darling in *Lost Girls*. You were superb!"

Lauren refrained from rolling her eyes at the other woman's praise. *Superb* was definitely overselling

Lauren as an actress, even if it had been a high school play.

The corner of Chase's mouth quirked up in amusement as he finished his cookie. "You didn't tell me you were a theater geek."

She shrugged. "I wasn't. Not really." She arched a playful brow his way. "If you haven't noticed, there aren't a lot of things for kids to do around here, which was why I took drama class my senior year."

"You were a *very* good actress," Betsy insisted. "And singer, too. Remember that karaoke contest you won at Jake's Pizzeria?"

Lauren groaned at the memory, feeling her cheeks warm in embarrassment. She'd just turned twenty-one, and after one too many cocktails she'd had enough liquid courage running through her veins to accept her friend's dare to sing "Baby One More Time". Yes, she'd commandeered the stage, complete with a bump and grind routine that had the crowd, and the boys, hooting and hollering and egging her on.

"Not really my finer moment," she said, ducking her head. "I was pretty toasted and way too uninhibited."

"I would have paid money to see that," Chase said, chuckling. "Look at you, so full of all these secret, hidden talents."

He was teasing her, of course, but his comment made Lauren think about what her sister had said to her. About how everything had come so easily for Lauren. She'd never thought of things that way before, or how inadequate her sister must have felt, even if it had been misplaced. It was crazy to her that they'd each had their own insecurities when it came to the other.

Betsy stood up. "Well, it's been nice chatting with you two, but I've got to head to the market and pick up a few things," she announced. "Would you like a lemonade or iced tea before I go, Lauren?"

She smiled at the other woman. "Iced tea would be great."

Betsy went into the adjoining kitchen and moments later, returned with a drink for Lauren, and then she was out the door, leaving her and Chase alone.

She took a sip of her sweetened tea and glanced at him, unable to miss how mellow he seemed to be, which she was grateful for. She wasn't sure what to expect after their earlier discussion about his turbulent past, then his pensive walk. She'd anticipated the possibility that he'd have erected those emotional walls again by the time he returned to the inn, or be in a more somber mood, but that wasn't the case.

"How did things go with your sister?" he asked as he absently wiped away the condensation on his glass with his long fingers. "Good, I hope?"

She nodded, then told him about her conversation with Ashley, about her sister's genuine apology, and how things really had gone down with Greg and their affair, and everything else they'd discussed. He listened intently, asked a few questions, and by the time she was done he had a gentle smile on his lips.

"I'm really glad you two made up and Ashley was honest about everything," he said, his voice low. "I'm sure your parents will be relieved and very happy to see you and your sister talking again, too."

"I know they will. The situation hasn't been easy on them, and I know they've been so conflicted and worried that Ashley and I would never repair our relationship." She took a drink of her tea before meeting his gaze and continuing. "They're going to the church a little early, since my dad is walking Ashley down the aisle, so I'm sure Ashley will tell them both about our talk today as soon as she sees them. For my parents, that will be the best gift ever, knowing that their daughters are back on speaking terms and no longer avoiding one another when they're in the same room."

"And what about Greg?" he asked, his eyes narrowing slightly and his voice turning gruff. "Are you going to be okay being in the same room with him?"

"Yes, of course," she said, surprised by that protective vibe Chase was giving off. "He'll be family after today, and I don't begrudge them their happiness."

"You're incredibly kind and empathetic," he murmured, lifting his hand and caressing the tips of his fingers along her cheek in a soft caress. "It's impressive, because those are qualities I haven't seen much of in my life."

The admission made her chest tighten with sadness for this damaged, broken man and everything he'd endured. "Being kind and empathetic isn't that hard.

It's all about being able to forgive people for the mistakes they've made, and I have."

She couldn't deny that the comment was also directed at him, at his situation with his father and all that resentment and bitterness she knew he still held on to over his childhood. Not to mention keeping Billie a secret to the very end of his life then dropping it on Chase like a bombshell. One conversation with her wasn't going to diminish those feelings, but she really hoped that Chase opened himself up to the possibility of forgiving his father, and letting go of things that were no longer in his control to change.

But that wasn't a discussion she wanted to have right now, not when she only had a short time left with him. And now that the uncomfortable tension between her and sister was gone, she was actually looking forward to the evening's festivities, and having fun at the reception with Chase.

She glanced at the time on her cellphone, realizing it was later than she'd thought. "I think we need to head upstairs to shower and get ready for the wedding," she suggested.

He nodded his agreement, and they went up to their room.

She opened her suitcase and sorted through her things, casting Chase a glance and giving him a playful grin. "I'd suggest taking a shower together to conserve water, but we saw how well that went this morning," she teased. "It took *twice* as long and we ran out of hot water. Not that I'm complaining, but time is of the essence this afternoon."

His eyes darkened with desire, as if remembering their sexcapades and all the dirty things he'd done to her with his mouth and his hands and his impressive cock. "As much as I hate to admit it, you're right," he said huskily, his voice tinged with regret. "We don't have an extra hour to mess around."

She silently mourned the loss of that hour of pleasure she was giving up, but the last thing she wanted to do was walk in late to her sister's wedding ceremony. Although wouldn't *that* stir up some juicy gossip in town, she thought with an inward grin.

Chase narrowed his gaze at her. "What are you smirking about?"

She couldn't help but provoke him, just a little. "Us, racing into the church, all flushed and out of breath from sex and orgasms and—"

"Stop tempting me," he said on a growl as he stalked toward her, looking heart-stoppingly sexy with that heated threat in his eyes that made her pulse race.

She laughed and held out her hand to stop his approach before they really did lose track of time. "Okay, okay, I'm sorry." As much as she enjoyed this more playful side to Chase, she forced her mind back to more pragmatic matters. "I'm going to take much longer in the bathroom since I have to do my hair and makeup, so why don't you go first?"

He did, and true to being a man, he was finished in less than twenty minutes. He walked out of the en suite, dark hair damp and his face freshly shaven, with nothing but a towel around his waist. Beads of water still clung to his chest, and she licked her lips as she watched one droplet roll its way down his abdomen and past his navel, imagining following that trail with her tongue and—

"Stop staring at me like that," he said in a gruff, tortured tone.

She jerked her gaze back up to his scowling face but did nothing to hide her unrepentant grin. "Sorry... not sorry," she said, continuing their light-hearted banter from earlier. "It's your own fault for walking around half naked," she tossed over her shoulder as she headed toward the bathroom, then enclosed herself inside.

Still smiling, she jumped into the shower. Over forty-five minutes later, her hair was dried and lightly curled, and she wore more makeup than she normally did since she knew she'd be taking family pictures after the wedding. She strolled back into the bedroom, mimicking Chase's earlier attire of just wearing a bath sheet wrapped around her body, the end tucked between her breasts to hold it in place.

He stood from where he'd been sitting on the small couch across the way, looking so gorgeous in a tailored, dark gray suit that fit his body to perfection. The sight of him stole her breath, and her stomach fluttered with awareness as she watched him approach, his gaze raking over her scantily clad figure before returning to her face.

He arched a dark, playfully accusing brow. "Oh,

and you berated *me* for walking around in nothing but a towel."

She blinked oh-so innocently at him. "I'd be more than happy to take it off." She reached for the knot between her breasts.

"Don't you fucking dare, because if you do I guarantee we *will* be late, and your hair and makeup will be ruined." He leaned close, his lips near her ear as he unraveled her with even more dirty talk. "But know that later, when we get back to this room, I'm going to dishevel the fuck out of you."

She shivered, feeling her nipples pebble against the towel. God, this man and his filthy mouth when they were alone was her undoing. This indecent side to him was such a contradiction to the gentleman he was in public, and she loved that she brought out this alpha, dominant side, and how desirable he made her feel.

"I'm going to hold you to that promise," she said, and turned toward the bed to grab the clothes she'd laid out to change into.

Except they weren't there. Instead, sitting on the comforter was a gray, glossy box with a pale pink ribbon wrapped around it.

Momentarily perplexed, she glanced at Chase, who still stood beside her. "Where are my clothes and what's this?" She waved a hand at the package.

He pushed his hands into the front pockets of his slacks. "*This* is what you're wearing tonight."

Confusion slid through her, and she went ahead and untied the ribbon and lifted the lid on the box.

Having no idea what to expect since there was no store name on the package, she peeled back the tissue and gasped at what she'd revealed—the beautiful lavender gown she'd seen in the window of Marie's boutique earlier that day. Alongside the dress was a pair of gray heels with sparkly straps to match the crystals that accentuated the ones on the shoulder of the gown.

Her throat grew tight. She was so incredibly touched that Chase had gone out of his way to surprise her with something so special, and undoubtedly expensive. "You shouldn't have," she whispered.

"I wanted to." He smiled, and lifting a hand, he gently caressed the pads of his fingers along her jawline, his eyes so warm and kind and caring she melted inside. "You deserve to have everything your heart desires."

Including you? she wanted to ask, but swallowed back the words because she didn't want to ruin this magical moment with such a serious question she might not like the answer to.

Instead, she ran her fingers across the silky, luxurious fabric, then met his gaze curiously. "How did you even know my size?"

"I have my ways." He gave her a sexy wink.

She could only assume he'd probably read the label on the dress she'd planned to wear tonight, and did it even really matter? The gift was so indulgent and told her just how much attention he'd paid to her today. She couldn't help but be overwhelmed by the thoughtful, sweet gesture and how this normally reserved, sedate man had gone out of his way to make her feel so treasured.

"Thank you," she said, her voice husky with emotion. "This means so much to me."

She closed the distance between them, and since she hadn't yet put on her lipstick, she raised up on her toes, grasped the lapels of his suit jacket, and placed her lips on his, kissing him softly. His hands went to her hips, and after a few lingering seconds she could feel him reluctantly lift his mouth from hers.

"You need to get dressed," he reminded her, the smile on his lips contradicting the spark of desire in his eyes.

Knowing he was right, she gathered up the box and took it with her into the bathroom. Ten minutes later she exited in the gown and heels—both a perfect fit—and the awestruck expression on Chase's face when he saw her was everything.

"Wow." His lips parted on a breath as he took in the way the fabric accentuated her curves, and how the slit up her left leg exposed her thigh and sparkling crystal shoes with every step she took. "You look stunningly gorgeous."

She stopped in front of him, and feeling a bit shy from his candid praise since she was unused to such overt compliments, she needlessly fixed his tie. "Thank you." She honestly felt like a goddess, and that wasn't something she'd ever thought of herself as before.

"Ready to go?" he asked, holding his arm out for

her to take.

Happy to have this handsome man by her side for the evening, she gave him a nod and placed her hand in the crook of his elbow. "Let's do this."

Chapter Thirteen

C HASE WALKED TOWARD the small church with
Lauren on his arm, an odd sense of pride filling
him when he caught the surreptitious stares cast their
way from some of the other guests gathered outside.
He didn't lie when he'd told Lauren she looked
stunningly gorgeous, and judging by the head-turning
glances from a few of the men in the area, it only
confirmed his earlier flattering remark.

"Let me introduce you to some of my family before we have to head inside," Lauren said, and guided
him toward where an elderly woman was waving them
over, her gaze brimming with interest as they landed
on him.

As soon as they reached the small congregation,
Lauren launched into introductions, acquainting him
with her aunts and uncles, numerous cousins, and
friends on her side of the family. They welcomed him
with friendly smiles and handshakes, complimented
Lauren on how beautiful she looked, and asked how
she was enjoying life in the big city.

Then, one of her aunts asked those questions everyone else was probably wondering, too, judging by

the curiosity in their eyes. How long have they been dating? Where did they meet? Where did he work and did he live in New York City, too?

He held Lauren's hand in his and took the other woman's interrogation in stride, and since he and Lauren had rehearsed the more personal questions, the answers came easily and seemed to appease everyone.

"We need to head inside and get seated," Lauren finally said, thankfully ending the inquisition.

They all entered the church. Since Lauren was immediate family, a groomsman ushered them to one of the front pews where her gramps was already seated. Chase shook the man's hand and Lauren gave him a kiss on the cheek, and then they settled in beside him. A short while later her mother, Penny, joined them after lighting the candles at the altar with Greg's mother.

The groom and his groomsmen took their places at the front, along with the bridesmaids. Light, lilting music began playing, and everyone stood up, so Chase followed suit, watching as Dale escorted his daughter down the aisle.

This was the first time Chase had ever seen Ashley, and while she was as beautiful as Lauren had said, he realized that the woman by his side was equally as radiant, and far more his type. Apparently, beauty queens didn't do it for him, and his strong attraction to Lauren was based on more than just her pretty face. He was beguiled by her lively spirit, determination, and optimistic attitude. He was impressed by the way she didn't take shit from him and hadn't let his grumpy personality deter her from getting what she wanted. Not many people stood up to Chase the way she had that day she'd come storming into his office, demanding he fulfill his bachelor auction obligation.

In an incredibly short amount of time, she'd bulldozed through all his defenses. Stripped away painful, emotional layers he'd safeguarded for most of his life. She'd provoked smiles and laughter when he rarely indulged in either. She exasperated him and amused him and challenged him, and those qualities were the things he was inexorably drawn to, despite knowing this was just a temporary, fake relationship for the sake of her having a date for the weekend. Knowing they'd be parting ways tomorrow afternoon made his chest tighten and ache in a way that was completely foreign to him.

He exhaled a deep breath and refocused his attention on the bride and groom. His thoughts had drifted to the point that he realized he'd missed most of the ceremony and vows, and they'd reached the part where the minister pronounced Greg and Ashley as husband and wife. The two kissed, everyone cheered, and down the aisle they went as a newly married couple.

"I need to stay for the family photos," Lauren said, turning to him as guests filed out of the pews and exited the church. "You're welcome to head to the reception with everyone else so you're not bored to tears here, and I can meet you there, if you'd like?"

He shook his head, because he knew that just

watching her do anything would never bore him. "No, I'll stay and wait for you."

A soft, appreciative smile curved her pink-tinted lips. "Such an attentive boyfriend," she whispered in a teasing voice, and brushed a light kiss across his cheek before she followed her parents and Gramps up to the altar.

The bride and groom returned shortly after, and Chase sat back down and watched as Lauren and Ashley exchanged a genuine hug and smiles. Greg was off to the side talking to an older gentleman who looked to be his father, so Lauren wasn't put in the position to have to converse with her ex for the time being.

While things were repaired with Ashley, Chase had no idea if the other man planned to follow suit and apologize to Lauren, as well. But Chase decided if Greg had any integrity at all, he'd fucking man up and express regret for his part in hurting Lauren.

For the duration of the photo session she and Greg never interacted, but Lauren was all smiles as the photographer took what seemed like endless amounts of pictures.

When Ashley's side of the family was finished, Lauren headed back to Chase and announced they were free to go. They drove his car to the reception and found a place to sit inside the venue, and it wasn't long before they were joined by her parents and Gramps, and then the bride and groom arrived, as well.

A delicious meal was served, speeches were made, and after dinner was finished, Ashley and Greg made their way around the room to greet their guests. Lauren and Chase had just stood from their table when the bride and groom approached. He slid his hand into Lauren's in a show of solidarity, and prepared to meet them for the first time.

Ashley's smile was sweet and kind, but Greg seemed uncomfortable in Lauren's presence. *Tough shit*, Chase thought.

"I wanted to make sure that we had a chance to meet Lauren's boyfriend before the evening gets too crazy," Ashley said, and extended her hand to him, which he gently shook. "It's so good to meet you."

"Pleasure to meet you as well," he replied in a warm, cordial tone.

"And this is Greg." Ashley smiled at her husband, as if to encourage him to do the polite thing and acknowledge their guest, as well.

Greg pulled back his shoulders as he reluctantly offered his hand. "Chase, right?"

"Yes." Chase didn't hesitate to clasp the other man's hand in a firm, tight grip. Maybe too tight and assertive, he thought, watching the way Greg winced—not that he gave a damn. "Congratulations to you both."

"Thank you," Ashley said, looping her arm through Greg's when Chase finally released his hand. "I hope you and Lauren have a nice evening."

The duo moved on, and as soon as they were out

of hearing distance, the cutest little giggle escaped Lauren. He glanced at her, realizing she'd already consumed two glasses of champagne, which probably accounted for her giddy mood.

"What?" he asked, wondering what had her so amused.

"I think you gripped Greg's hand a little *too* hard, being all dominant and alpha with him," she said, stepping up to him and sliding her arms around his neck, not caring who saw them. "Which, admittedly, I found kind of hot."

"You saw that, did you?" He smirked, wrapping his own hands around her waist and enjoying the warmth of her body aligned with his. "He needs to up his handshake game. It was a little too soft."

She gave him a sultry look that made his dick twitch in his slacks, as did the way she pressed one hand to his chest then slowly stroked downward. "Well, we know there's *nothing* soft about you," she said huskily.

He groaned at her brazen display and grabbed her wrist before those fingers traveled into inappropriate territory. "You're a little tipsy."

She tossed her head back and laughed, not denying his claim, then grinned at him. "Let's go take some silly pictures in the photo booth."

Doing something so frivolous wasn't his thing, and while he'd normally refuse, he found he didn't want to disappoint her. Then again, the way she grabbed his hand and dragged him over to the booth didn't give him much of an option, either.

As they waited their turn to sit inside the cubicle, she selected a few props and sayings attached to a stick from the side table. By the time they made it to the front of the line, she had a handful of accessories.

They slipped inside the small, enclosed space, Lauren closed the black curtain for privacy, and then they both settled in side by side on the very small bench seat. Lauren handed him a few of the cutouts, and with a press of a button the camera started flashing in intervals, giving them just enough time to swap out the various props and sayings and strike a new pose.

In the first snapshot, she held up "I came for the cake", while he raised a "life of the party", phrase, his brows arched comically, because that was the last thing he was. They went through everything she'd brought inside, using the moustache, tiara, heart-shaped glasses, and top hat interchangeably with each other, along with all the ridiculous expressions and outlandish gestures she goaded out of him.

Her laughter throughout the five-minute session was infectious, curling through him and inciting his own chuckles, too.

Between the last few shots, she jumped up and settled herself across his lap, staring at him with a frisky grin as she framed his face in her hands. For a brief moment, she stopped and just looked at him, her expression softening as their eyes met, just long enough for the camera to capture the moment on film. The bright illumination seemed to jolt her back to reality, and that playful nature of hers reappeared as she kissed him.

The second their lips touched he forgot where they were. Forgot everything but this woman who'd shaken up his neat and orderly world and had coaxed him to just let loose and fucking enjoy the moment.

With a groan, he slid his hand around to the nape of her neck, deepening the kiss and oblivious to the final click of the camera. She returned his efforts with fervor, and Christ, she tasted so sweet and hot he couldn't get enough of her.

The slit in her dress exposed one leg, and he caressed his free hand up her thigh, his thumb caressing her soft, silky skin. She made a small, inarticulate sound in the back of her throat and squirmed on his lap, causing the movement of her ass to rub against the fly of his pants, making his cock thicken.

Someone rapped on the side of the cubicle, jarring them apart.

"Hey, that's not a make-out booth," a humorous male voice said from the other side of the curtain.

Fuck. How in the hell had he gotten so carried away at a public venue? Sexy, reckless *Lauren*, that's how. "We'll be out in a second," Chase said, hoping that would be enough time for his dick to calm the fuck down.

"We, umm, just need to input our phone numbers for the photos," she said to the man, sounding as breathless as she looked, with her lips a bit swollen from their kiss and her cheeks flushed with desire.

She looked at him again and giggled adorably, uncaring that they'd been caught. Then she shifted her attention to the monitor on the panel in front of them and punched in her number.

"You need to behave," he growled into her ear.

She shivered, a naughty glimmer in her eyes as they met his. "What's the fun in that?"

Yeah, he couldn't deny it *had* been fun. He just shook his head, but he was grinning as he added his digits to the keypad so he'd get his own set of digital photos.

She pushed to her feet, straightening the lower part of her gown so that the slit didn't show off as much skin, which he appreciated since he didn't want any other man staring at her legs. He stood beside her in the cramped space, and still wearing his jacket, he fastened the button, which helped to conceal the stiff bulge in his slacks.

They exited the booth to find that it was Lauren's cousin, Richard, who'd interrupted their kiss, and had to endure a bit more teasing from him. With their time spent at the photo booth, they'd missed the cake cutting, but unfortunately they were just in time for the DJ to announce the bouquet and garter toss.

Lauren threaded her fingers in his and pulled him toward the dance floor, where everyone was starting to gather. "Considering it's my sister's wedding, and I'm single, I should probably join the bouquet toss." She glanced at him, a daring light in her eyes. "And it wouldn't hurt if you participated in the garter toss, since you're single and we're technically dating."

Oh, for fuck's sake. Everything in him wanted to protest, because how goddamn awkward was it to stand around with a bunch of other guys who were eagerly vying for the bride's garter?

Ashley tossed a small floral arrangement of roses first, and how ironic was it that it went straight for Lauren, giving her no choice but to put up her hands and catch the bundle of flowers or it would have smacked her right in the chest. The women around her clapped and cheered, and Ashley hugged her, seemingly happy that it was her sister that had caught the bouquet.

The men were called out onto the dance floor next, and despite the dread settling in the pit of his stomach, Chase sucked up his discomfort and joined the other single males. He just made damn sure he stood *way* off to the side, purposely avoiding the line of fire, and his strategy worked. One of Greg's groomsmen jumped up in the air and caught the garter, with Chase nowhere near the danger zone.

He met back up with Lauren, walking with her to their table so she could set her flowers down. She sighed and smiled up at him as the lights were dimmed and the DJ coaxed everyone out onto the dance floor and started playing an upbeat tune.

"I have to say, it's nice being on the other side of an event as a guest, instead of being the one who planned it and is dashing around making sure everything is running smoothly," she said, referencing her job as an event planner at the Meridian. "Don't get me wrong, I love my job, but it's nice not having to worry about anything and just have a good time."

"I'm glad you're enjoying yourself," he said, and he meant it.

A sly grin replaced her languid smile, and a mischievous look sparked in her eyes. "Speaking of which, let's go dance."

He adamantly shook his head, because this was where he drew the line. "Yeah… no. I don't dance. But I see your girl cousins and friends out there dancing together, so you go and have fun."

"I don't want to leave you by yourself." She pouted, and as endearing as the gesture was, it did nothing to change his mind.

"I'll be fine," he insisted, and jutted his chin toward the dance area. "Go."

One of her cousins called Lauren's name and waved her over, and she finally gave in and joined them, letting loose her inhibitions on the dance floor.

Chase might not like to dance, but he quickly learned that he *loved* watching Lauren move her hips and shake her ass to the beat of the music.

Chapter Fourteen

MUCH TO CHASE'S surprise, the next few hours passed quickly and enjoyably. While Lauren danced her little heart out, he nursed a drink and chatted a bit with her father, Dale, and a few of her male cousins. He honestly thought the time would drag on, or he'd feel out of place, but that wasn't the case. Lauren's family was warm and welcoming, and when he wasn't conversing with someone, his date completely captured his attention.

She spent most of her time out on the dance floor with her single friends, her face flushed from all the physical activity, and her hair a bit of a disheveled mess, which only made her look sexier. But her eyes were bright and she was laughing and smiling as the group of women, along with Ashley, did the Macarena, which involved more of that hip swiveling and an enticing bounce of her breasts as she jumped in place then clapped her hands before starting the choreographed moves all over again.

So, yeah, he was far from bored. In fact, dare he say he even had a perma-smile on his face, that's how much he was enjoying himself. *Shocker.*

"A little shy at the garter toss earlier, wouldn't you say?" her gramps asked, sidling up to where Chase was standing at the far side of the room.

He'd been so mesmerized by Lauren that he hadn't seen Lee approach, but he turned his head and smiled at the older man, who had a speculative gleam in his eye. Of course the wily old man would notice his reluctance, and had no qualms about calling him out on it.

Chase shrugged nonchalantly. "I don't need to catch a garter to know when and if I'm going to get married." Which had always been a hard *never* for him.

Lee chuckled. "Fair enough." He glanced out to the dance floor, grinning when he saw his granddaughter now rocking out to the cult classic "Tequila" song, and yelling out the one-word lyric, "Tequila!" with everyone else on cue. "I have to say, my girl looks happier than I've seen her in a very long time."

Chase had taken his suit jacket off a while ago and now he pushed his hands into the front pocket of his slacks. "It's the whole wedding thing," he said to explain away Lauren's emotional and mental well-being. "It puts people in a festive mood."

Lee scoffed and narrowed his gaze at Chase. "Don't sell yourself short. There is no doubt in my mind that you're the reason that smile of hers has finally reached her eyes. I was worried it was gone for good, but it just took the *right* man to bring it back."

Chase swallowed hard, hating that tight feeling in his chest, because he was far from being the *right man* for Lauren. No, he was all wrong for her, because she deserved someone who was whole and complete and not emotionally unavailable like him. A man who didn't have the first clue how to make a relationship work and last, and would probably fuck it all up if he tried and ended up hurting her.

There was no denying they shared a strong connection, but it was hard for Chase to fathom that he could be responsible for all that joy she exuded, or even a fraction of it. Then again, wasn't she the reason *he* felt lighter inside?

Not wanting Lee to start asking questions Chase didn't have the answers for, he instead diverted the conversation before it became any more personal. "Would you like a beer or something else from the bar?" he asked, watching as Lauren walked off the dance floor with one of her cousins and headed toward the ladies' room.

"No. Beer is for pansies, and all they have at that bar is the cheap crap that tastes like piss. I brought the good stuff." Lee reached into the inside pocket of his suit jacket and retrieved a silver flask.

The corner of Chase's mouth twitched with amusement, because Lee was right. The alcohol the bar was serving was far from the top-shelf premium liquor he was used to drinking. "The good stuff?" he asked, curious to know what the older man had smuggled into the reception.

Lee nodded. "Yep. You can't go wrong with Elijah Craig, barrel proof."

Definitely a higher-end bourbon, and one Chase had appreciated more than a few times himself. "You have good taste."

"Of course I do," Lee said, and chuckled. "But don't tell Penny that I snuck some into the reception. A man has to have a few vices to live for."

Chase grinned as Lee took a swig of the liquor. "Not a word. You have my promise."

Lee smacked his lips and after recapping the flask, he tucked it back inside his jacket. "So, have you taken Scouty to that fancy restaurant she's been wanting to go to in the city? In Manhattan, I think it is."

The older man was looking at him expectantly, like Chase ought to know what he was talking about, but of course he didn't. "Which restaurant would that be?"

The lines between Lee's brows crinkled as he tried to remember the name, and then his eyes lit up and he snapped his fingers. "Elysian Heights," he finally said. "Some top chef on a cooking show runs it. She said it just opened in the past year but it's nearly impossible to get a table. Just thought you would have been able to pull some strings and make that happen. I mean, you *are* a partner in an investment firm in New York City, so that ought to come with some kind of perks."

At least the old man hadn't called him a *fancy pants* this time, but the inference was there just the same. And there was no way Chase was going to admit that he'd taken a client to Elysian Heights just a month ago because Chase had an "in" with the owner of the restaurant, another client of his. "I didn't realize

Lauren wanted to go there," he said, which was the truth.

Lee frowned at Chase, eyeing him speculatively, considering he was supposed to be her boyfriend and know these things. "Huh. I'm surprised she didn't mention it. She's talked about it the few times she's been home this past year."

Much to Chase's relief, Lee let the subject go and glanced away, his gaze scanning the last of the wedding guests at the winding-down reception. "Well, would you look over there," he said suddenly, rocking back on his heels. "I think that's the first time I've seen Greg and Lauren standing that close together since everything went down a few years ago."

That caught Chase's attention, and he followed the direction to where Lee was staring. The lights in the room were still dimmed, but he could see that Greg had probably caught Lauren as she'd come out of the ladies' room, and while Ashley was still on the dance floor. Lauren had proven more than once that she was capable of taking care of herself, but there was no denying the possessive feeling that stirred inside of him. He wanted to be by her side and offer the kind of support she'd given him earlier that afternoon.

"Excuse me," he said to Lee, not missing the other man's amused look before he strode across the room, reaching the pair in less than a minute.

Lauren sucked in a startled breath as he slid his arm around her waist and pulled her close to his side. "Everything okay here?" he asked in a commanding tone. Yeah, interrupting them was probably a dick move, but he didn't give a shit. What he *did* care about was Lauren, and making sure she wasn't subjected to anything that might upset her or hurt her in any way.

Greg had a deer-in-the-headlights look in his eyes, clearly not sure what to make of Chase and his territorial gesture. Or his presence in general. "I... uh, just wanted to talk to Lauren. Privately," Greg added.

Chase didn't budge, waiting for Lauren to decide what *she* wanted.

She lifted her chin and leaned in closer to him, accepting his silent encouragement. "He can stay," she said in a confident tone. "Whatever you have to say to me isn't anything Chase doesn't already know."

"Okay." Greg nodded, his complexion ruddy with embarrassment. "So, Ashley told me she came over earlier to the inn to apologize, and I know it's been two years and this conversation is long overdue. I wanted to say that I'm sorry, as well, for the way things happened. It was wrong, and if I had the chance to do it over again, I definitely would have handled things differently between you and I."

"How so?" she asked.

The fact that Lauren didn't just let Greg off the hook with immediate forgiveness surprised Chase, and he was proud of her for holding the man accountable for his part in what had transpired between them.

Greg shifted anxiously on his feet. "I think we both knew that our relationship wasn't as strong as it should have been, that we'd been... growing apart," he said, echoing what Lauren had told Chase, as well. "But the bottom line is, I should have ended things with you before starting anything with Ashley. I hate that I hurt you."

"Thank you. For your honesty and your apology," she said, standing firm beside Chase. "Finding you and Ashley together did hurt at the time, because I was blindsided, but I can look past all that and know that things worked out for the best. You seem very happy with my sister, and I never would have moved to New York and found a job I absolutely love."

Greg's mouth quirked in a smile as he finally started to relax, and his gaze flickered to Chase. "Or a man who clearly appreciates you, the way you deserve."

"He's been a nice little bonus," she agreed in a teasing tone, meeting Chase's gaze for a few seconds, looking truly grateful that he was there with her, before glancing back at Greg. "As for you and Ashley and I, I just want us all to move forward with a clean slate."

Relief etched the other man's features. "I would like that, too. Very much."

"Consider it done," she said easily.

He exhaled a deep breath, probably glad that the discussion was over, and glanced over Lauren's shoulder to the dance floor. "I'm going to go and find Ashley before the evening ends."

Greg left the two of them, and Chase turned toward Lauren, tipping her chin up with his fingers so he could get a good look at her face and see her eyes, which were bright and clear. "How are you doing?" he asked, just to check in with her. He didn't want to assume anything after a difficult conversation like that.

She stepped closer and slid her arms around his waist, her smile as authentic and real as the woman herself as she looked up at him. "I'm doing great."

"Good." He was truly glad that things would be much easier for her and the entire family moving forward.

The DJ announced the last song of the night, encouraging the people who were still at the reception to join the bride and groom on the dance floor as he played a final slow, romantic ballad.

"Come on, let's go dance," Chase said spontaneously, watching as her eyes widened in surprise, then happiness at his suggestion.

Before she could say anything, he grabbed her hand and led her out to the wooden platform, where even her mom and dad were enjoying the final melody. He pulled her into his embrace, securing one arm tight around her waist and lacing his fingers with hers.

Lauren arched a playful brow at him. "I thought you said you didn't dance," she accused him in soft tone.

"I don't *fast* dance," he clarified, bringing their bodies together as intimately as possible in a public setting. "This, though, is easy. All I have to do is hold you close and shuffle around the dance floor."

She smiled up at him. "I like being this close to you," she said, then laid her head on his shoulder.

Those words unraveled something deep inside him, and he swallowed hard, because he liked being this close to her, too. So damn much. To the point that he never wanted to let her go.

He closed his eyes and breathed her in, imprinting this moment in his memory as they moved together slowly, their thighs brushing and other body parts rubbing intimately as they swayed to the slow beat of the music.

Each moment that passed, the awareness and sensual tension between them climbed. He could feel Lauren's breathing change and escalate, and those damp gusts of air that slipped past her parted lips warmed his neck and aroused him. He couldn't ignore the way she subtly, but deliberately bumped her pelvis against his, wreaking havoc with his self-control as she slowly gyrated her hips, reminding him of just how uninhibited this woman was when it came to sex.

Right before the song ended, she lifted her head from his shoulder and whispered in his ear. "I'm ready to head back to the inn. How about you?" she asked, her meaning obvious.

"Yes," he agreed, because he was *beyond* desperate to be alone with her.

She pulled back just enough for him to see the seductive smile on her lips. "Then what are you waiting for? I believe you promised to dishevel the fuck out of me, and I'm so ready for that."

He groaned at those filthy, unfiltered words coming from her mouth, completely turned on that she could be so straightforward with him about what she wanted. "So am I," he growled in a low voice.

She bit her bottom lip, the desire in her eyes unmistakable. "Then take me home and fuck me."

A surge of lust rippled through him, and much to his relief, moments later the song ended, because he was *this close* to hoisting her over his shoulder and carrying her out of the venue like an uncivilized caveman. They made the rounds and said their good-byes, which was the right and appropriate thing to do, but all Chase could think about was getting Lauren naked and burying his cock inside her, as deep as he could get.

The drive back to the inn was short, thank God, but that didn't stop Lauren from leaning over the console as much as her seat belt would allow so she could slide her hand up his thigh and trail her fingers over the fly of his slacks. She whispered dirty things in his ear that heated his blood, then kissed and licked the side of his neck while palming and stroking his hard-as-a-rock dick through his pants. She was so bold and brazen and shameless, and he fucking loved it.

As they rushed into the inn after that bit of fore-play in the car, Chase was grateful it was late and that Betsy, or anyone else, wasn't up to watch the way he grabbed Lauren's hand and impatiently dragged her up the stairs with him. He heard her soft, sultry laughter, but she didn't lag behind, clearly just as eager for this tryst as he was.

The second they stepped into their room and the

door was closed and locked behind them, Lauren reached behind her to unzip her gown, while he toed off his shoes. They'd left the bedside lamp on when they'd left earlier so they'd have some light when they returned, and that's all the illumination they needed.

When the silky lavender fabric dropped to the floor, she stepped out of the dress and approached him in a sexy-as-fuck lacy bra and matching panties that were a shimmering beige, those crystals heels still on her feet. It was all he could do *not* to bend her over the bed, strip her underwear to her thighs, and slam into her from behind, taking her right then and there.

She eagerly shoved his suit jacket off his shoulders while he loosened his tie and tossed it aside, the haste to get each other naked a wild and uncontrollable thing. He got rid of his cuff links as she started unfastening his shirt, her movements hurried, but a small sound of frustration escaped her lips when she kept fumbling with a particularly stubborn button.

She glanced up at him, her impatience obvious in her expression. "God, I just want to rip your damn shirt off."

He found himself grinning as he remembered what she'd told him, how she'd had no urge to tear off her ex's clothes because of the lack of passion between them. This moment spoke to her unbridled need and the urgency between *them*, and he wasn't about to deprive her of something so provocative and sexy.

And *fun*, he realized. Something he'd never indulged in during sex, but felt so right with this woman who was always so playful and spirited.

He grabbed her fumbling hands and positioned them where the shirt was open right above that stubborn button. "Go ahead and do it," he urged her huskily. "Rip my shirt open."

He eyes widened in shock at his command, and then she quickly shook her head, sending her silky hair cascading across her bare shoulders. "I can't do that! This shirt probably cost a small fortune."

The garment had been pricey, but he didn't give a damn. "Yeah, you can," he said, and curled her fingers around the fabric so that she was now gripping it in her fists. "I want all that passion, baby. Give it to me."

She bit her bottom lip, and he loved the way her eyes lit up as she gave in to temptation and pulled the sides apart, hard and fast, sending buttons flying in different directions and shredding his shirt apart in less than three seconds.

She laughed in delight as she shoved the shirt off him. "Oh, my God. That was *so* hot."

He chuckled, too, as he quickly unbuckled his belt and shucked off his pants and boxer briefs. Once he was naked, she placed her hands on his chest and guided him back a few steps, bypassing the bed and continuing toward the small couch situated in the sitting area a short distance away.

"Sit down while I get a condom," she ordered.

Her bossy tone amused him, and for now he let her take control. He settled on the sofa, watching as she retrieved a few condoms and came back, tossing them onto the seat beside him. When he reached for one to put it on, she stopped him.

"Not yet," she said, a wicked gleam in her eye as her gaze lowered to his erect and already aching cock.

He arched a brow and gave an order of his own. "Take off the rest of your lingerie. I want you just as naked as I am."

"I'm getting there," she chided playfully, then proceeded to give him a slow, tantalizing strip show.

First, she unclasped her bra and let it slide down her arms and drop to the floor at her feet. He stared at those small, firm, perfect breasts, his mouth watering for a taste he knew he'd soon get, before he let his gaze drift lower, to where she was shimmying out of her panties. When they pooled around her ankles, she stepped out of them, but didn't proceed to remove her sparkly, crystal heels.

"I love the shoes, so they stay on," she said, almost impishly.

He raised his eyes back up to her face, enjoying the view along the way. He didn't argue because after she was done running this particular part of the show, he planned to fuck her with those sexy heels on, with her legs over his shoulders and those spiky heels dragging across his back.

He expected her to climb onto his lap, but instead she lowered to her knees in front of him. She pushed his legs apart and moved in between, her eyes on his stiff cock. The muscles in his abdomen clenched as her palms skimmed up his thighs and she leaned forward, momentarily closing her eyes as she licked a slow, gradual path up the length of his shaft until she reached the tip.

Her tongue flicked over the crown and he groaned, his cock pulsing as she did it again, returning to the base of his erection and teasing him with another leisurely taste. He caught the mischievous smile she was trying to hide, and the next time she licked him like a lollipop and reached the top, he slid a hand into her hair, tightened his fingers around the strands, and took back a semblance of control.

"Open your pretty mouth so I can fuck it," he rasped.

Eyes on him, she wrapped her fingers around his erection and parted her lips over the head of his cock. He inhaled a sharp breath as she enveloped him in her warm, wet mouth, taking him all the way to her throat, then back up again. Her hand followed in firm strokes up and down his shaft, and it wasn't long before he was guiding her head a little faster, a little deeper, while she sucked him harder, squeezed his dick tighter, and pushed him to the brink of insanity in no time flat.

He swore out loud, and gripping her hair, he pulled her mouth off of him. She made a disappointed sound in the back of her throat, as if she would have happily sucked him off, and he shook his head and exhaled harshly.

"As good as that feels, I want to come inside you while you're riding my cock," he rasped, untangling his fingers from her hair, now completely disheveled from his manhandling. "As deep as I can get."

Desire sparked in her eyes, and while she stood, he quickly sheathed his cock with the condom. Then, grabbing her hips, he pulled her forward. She straddled his lap and reached between them, dragging the head of his shaft through her slick arousal before positioning the sensitive head right against her core, taking him one excruciating inch inside of her before stopping.

Her hands moved to his shoulders, and her eyes met his. "Do it," she whispered on a sultry dare. "Fuck me, as deep as you can go."

Jesus. With his fingers still digging into her hips, he jerked her down, hard and fast, until he was seated to the hilt inside her. She gasped at the initial shock of him filling her full, then as her body adjusted around him, she dropped her head back, moaned and started to move on him.

He watched her, enraptured by the sinuous way she arched her back and gyrated her hips, and the tempting bounce of her breasts as she rode his cock before grinding down on him to create friction against her clit. He skimmed his palms along the indentation of her waist and continued upward, until he reached her breasts. Taking them in his hands, he squeezed the soft flesh and plucked her stiff peaks, eliciting a soft cry of pleasure from her lips. Then, he soothed that sting with his tongue, licking then lightly, sucking her nipples until whimpers of need filled the air between them.

He raised his hands to her face, tipping her head

forward and watching as she opened her eyes, meeting his gaze and giving him a glimpse of warmth, affection, and so much passion. The connection between them was raw and real, unlike anything he'd ever experienced, and his heart thundered in his chest at the knowledge of just how much Lauren meant to him. Physical pleasure was a given between them, but he hadn't counted on the emotional component of how this woman made him feel. *More alive than he had in years.*

But knowing that realization changed nothing after tonight, he focused on this moment with her and the way she moved on him a little faster as she chased her own orgasm. Her lips parted as her breathing escalated, along with the frantic way she fucked herself on his cock, and then her lashes fluttered closed as he felt the tension inside of her begin to unravel.

"Look at me, baby," he ordered huskily, still holding her flushed face in his hands, his own body taut beneath hers and ready to follow her over the peak. "I want to feel it all, and I want to look into your eyes as you come for me."

She opened her eyes, staring into his as the last tendrils of her release broke free. Deep and intense, the orgasm quaked through her and pulsed around his shaft, the pleasure almost unbearable as she splintered apart with a soft cry of bliss. He grunted as he thrust up into her, bringing her mouth to his. He claimed her with a deep, possessive, tongue-tangling kiss as he surrendered to his own explosive release, coming long and hard, until she'd wrung him dry and he had nothing left to give.

Especially not the kind of promises she deserved.

She collapsed against his chest, and he wrapped his arms around her and held her close, his hands stroking up and down her back while he imprinted everything about her to memory.

Because by this time tomorrow evening, she would no longer be his.

Chapter Fifteen

O N THE DRIVE home the following afternoon, during a lull in the light, superficial conversation between her and Chase, Lauren turned her head and stared at the NYC skyline coming into view. As happy as she was to be home, she dreaded the moment she and Chase would part ways.

And she knew they would. She'd woken up that morning alone in bed, Chase already in the shower. Even after he walked out of the bathroom—fully dressed—he'd gone downstairs to get them coffee and a light breakfast, to "give her some privacy" to get ready herself.

After everything that had transpired between them, what the hell was up with that? A stupid question, because she knew it was Chase's way of putting distance between them, creating a tangible and jarring shift from the man who'd made love to her the night before, and the connection they'd established over the last few days. Instead, he'd re-erected his emotional walls and it hurt to the core considering how much they'd shared over the course of the weekend.

Not just sex, which had been the best she'd ever

had, but their deep, intimate discussions, and the way they'd both been vulnerable enough to open up about different parts of their past. She understood how painful his childhood had been, and how that had impacted his adult life, and she'd foolishly hoped that maybe she'd given him a reason to believe in them. That together, they had something worth fighting for.

Instead, after he'd returned with coffee, fruit, and some muffins on a tray, he stated that he'd wanted to get an early start on the drive home. He started packing up things and loading the car like he couldn't get out of there fast enough. That's when she knew it was over, without the need for conversation. He'd fulfilled his obligation as her weekend boyfriend, and they really were going to go their separate ways.

Her heart ached but she reminded herself that he hadn't made her any promises. In fact, he'd been painfully upfront and clear about his inability to be anything more than a temporary diversion and affair. *"...the reality is, I don't do long term because I don't know how. I don't do commitments because I don't have that ability. I can't make you the kind of promises someone like you deserves."*

Clearly, despite everything, those words still held true, and she'd been stupid to believe she could have been the one to pry open his heart and show him everything *he* deserved.

She closed her eyes and breathed deep, remembering the conversation she'd had with her mother the night before at the reception. About how much her parents really liked Chase, and how they couldn't wait for them to come and visit again.

"I just want to say, this weekend is the happiest I've seen you in years and it fills my heart with so much joy," her mother had said, as she gently touched Lauren's cheek. *"I see the way Chase has watched you this entire evening, the way he looks at you like he truly adores you…"*

Lauren swallowed hard. If only that were true, then she'd be sitting beside a different man. One who hadn't given her every indication he was about to let her go. A man who would have fought for her.

But despite everything, Chase was a good guy. A victim of a shitty upbringing that had skewed his views on relationships and commitment to a woman, but still a solid, honorable man.

As she felt his car make the familiar turns and stops toward her apartment building, the pain in her chest increased. And since Chase hadn't mentioned seeing her again, she resigned herself to the reality of their situation. This was the end.

The vehicle came to a stop. The engine shut off, and Lauren forced her eyes back open, glancing at Chase, determined to keep things amicable despite her feeling so shattered inside.

"Thank you for standing in as my boyfriend for the weekend. I appreciate it." She hated how imper-sonal her words sounded, but she didn't know what else to say.

He gave her a very poor attempt at a smile. "I think the weekend accomplished what you needed for your family."

"Yes, it did," she agreed, and for that, she was grateful.

She got out of the car, and he did the same, meeting up with her at the trunk where he pulled out her luggage.

"So, what are you going to tell your parents about us?" he asked, his voice low, somber even.

He was referring to their *inevitable breakup*. She shrugged, trying to remain indifferent when her emotions were a tangled mess in her chest. "That things didn't work out. People break up all the time."

He nodded, and she could see the conflict in his eyes. The pained expression on his face told her that he was having as difficult a time letting her go as she was with walking away.

She'd never been the type of woman to beg and plead for a man to want her. But she realized she couldn't leave Chase without telling him how she truly felt about him—even knowing it wouldn't change his decision.

She cleared her throat. "There's something I want you to know, Chase," she said, holding his gaze. "I care about you. In fact, I'm halfway in love with you."

He groaned, sounding like a man tortured. "Lauren—"

She cut him off and rushed on, not wanting to hear his platitudes. "I hope you don't come to regret letting go of something that has the potential to make you happy. You might not think you're capable of being happy, but I've seen it this weekend. I felt it. I lived it with you because you made *me* happy, too." She stepped up to him and placed a soft kiss on his cheek. "I wish it could have been different for us. Goodbye, Chase."

His jaw clenched, turmoil swirling in the depths of his eyes, but when he didn't say anything in return, she grabbed the handle of her luggage and followed the walkway leading up to her building.

At the beginning of this past weekend with Chase, she'd promised to keep her heart out of the equation, but that was before she'd seen the man beneath the façade he put up for the rest of the world. And that man had been impossible to resist.

FOR WHAT FELT the dozenth time, Chase attempted to review the prospectus on his computer screen, seeing the financial and investment data, but his brain was having a hard time retaining the information. Which was a problem, when he needed to assess whether this particular investment aligned with his client's financial goals and risk tolerance.

He groaned in frustration at his inability to concentrate and sat back in his leather chair, rubbing his fingers across his forehead. Being distracted was par for the course the past four days, since watching Lauren walk away from him while struggling internally with all the foreign emotions waging war inside of him. There had been panic and dread at the thought of never seeing her again, and worse was the hurt he'd seen in her eyes because causing her pain was the last thing he'd ever intended to do.

And then there was the crushing amount of regret he couldn't shake, no matter how hard he'd tried. Telling himself he'd done the right thing was a fucking bitter pill to swallow, especially when he was miserable without her.

Chase wasn't a man who'd harbored a lot of regrets in his life. Even as a child, when his mother had walked out without so much as a goodbye and his own father had been emotionally and mentally unavailable, Chase had done whatever it had taken to survive and get himself to the point where he only had to think about himself.

Having two absentee parents had forced him to grow up fast. That lack of unconditional love and guidance throughout his formative years had taught him to rely only on himself, to the exclusion of forming emotional attachments with others because he refused to live through that kind of painful disappointment ever again.

He'd held on to so much bitterness over his mother's abandonment, and then his father's choice to drown his sorrow in self-pity and alcohol, to the point that those two major blows in Chase's life had driven him to make sure he became a stronger, more accomplished man than his dad ever was.

Chase had always believed that the anger and resentment pushing him forward made him stronger because it meant no one could hurt him or make him feel so isolated and *less than* ever again. And maybe, at one point in his life, those emotions had served their purpose to shape him into the successful man he was. But now... that lingering anger and resentment made him feel weak, because he was too fucking afraid to open up to a woman who gave him so much hope for a future he'd never allowed himself to even consider.

He'd always been of the mind that he couldn't change the past, so there was no sense in wallowing in regrets and wishing that things had turned out differently. Mostly because the situation he'd been dealt when it came to his parents hadn't been within his control.

But losing Lauren had been based on *his* decision. His actions. He was responsible for being exactly where he was, *alone again*, having lost a woman who'd not only pierced his emotional armor, but had given him the sweetest glimpse of what it felt like to have it all.

Instead, he'd been a martyr, so fucking convinced letting her go had been noble, because really, how could a vivacious woman like her fall in love with a broken man like him, one who knew nothing about deep, unconditional love? And now, he just felt hollow inside because he missed Lauren. Her sassy and mischievous personality and her optimistic outlook on life, despite what had happened with her ex. The way she made him smile and laugh and not take life too seriously when he was with her. How she'd been able to forgive her sister for what had happened between them.

And now, when he closed his eyes, he couldn't stop seeing her standing at the curb when he'd dropped her off four days ago, her heart so open and vulnerable as she told him how happy he'd made *her* that weekend. How was that even possible?

Chase's chest tightened as he replayed Lauren's last words to him in his mind, each one a piercing reminder of how he'd failed her. He'd spent years building walls to protect himself, but now he saw them for what they truly were… barriers to love, to happiness, and everything that mattered.

And Lauren, he realized, mattered most of all. But was he ready to try with her? And if he was, how in the hell did he repair the damage he'd done?

The vibration of his cellphone indicated he had a text notification. The sound startled him out of his thoughts, and he picked up the cell. The message was from Billie, who he hadn't seen or spoken to since his weekend with Lauren. He paused before opening the text, wondering if his sister somehow knew what occurred between him and Lauren and intended to interrogate him via text.

Dread settled into a hard knot in his stomach, and he swiped open the message to read what she'd written.

How about meeting me for dinner tonight at Luigi's? There's someone I want you to meet.

He frowned at the cryptic message, though he was

relieved that her text wasn't about Lauren. He hated to think how disappointed Billie would be with him if she knew how badly he'd fucked things up with her friend.

Exhaling a deep breath, he welcomed the distraction of eating dinner out so he didn't have to spend another evening alone in his too quiet apartment, immersed in depressing thoughts.

He replied with, *That sounds good. Make reservations for 6pm, and I'll see you there.*

The rest of the afternoon passed painfully slow, but at least Chase managed to finish the prospectus he'd been reviewing and gave Victoria his notes to type up into a professional-sounding letter with all his recommendations for his client.

At twenty to six, Chase left the office and drove a few blocks to the Italian place that was one of his sister's favorite restaurants, more than a little curious to find out who this mystery person was that Billie wanted him to meet, and why.

Chase arrived first, and the hostess brought him to their table. He took a seat so he was facing the entrance, and a few minutes later the same woman escorted Billie and a man he'd never seen before to where he was waiting.

He stood up and gave his sister a hug. As she stepped back out of his embrace, he couldn't miss her radiant smile and the sparkle of happiness in her eyes behind her black framed glasses. Billie was always cheerful and bubbly, but he had a feeling her guest was the one responsible for her added exuberance, if the other man's look of adoration toward Billie was any indication.

Interesting.

"Chase, I'd like you to meet Neil Pierson," she said, introducing him to the gentleman standing next to her, who looked well put together in a navy business suit, wire-rimmed glasses, and appeared to be in his early twenties, close in age to Billie. "Neil, this is my brother, Chase."

"It's a pleasure to finally meet you," Neil said, shaking Chase's hand in a firm grip. "Billie has told me so much about you. All good things, I assure you," he joked with an easygoing grin.

Chase smiled back. "Good to know. Have a seat," he said, indicating the other two vacant chairs at the table.

Neil held out Billie's chair for her, impressing Chase with his social graces when it came to treating women with respect. She thanked Neil, a pink flush sweeping across her cheeks.

They settled in and ordered their meals, and once the waiter had delivered their glasses of wine, Chase glanced across the table at the pair, noticing the way Neil held Billie's hand on top of the table, not hiding his affection for her.

Chase had no reason to dislike the man, but he had to admit he was feeling a bit protective of Billie. This was the first time she'd ever introduced him to a boyfriend, so he assumed that things between the two had to be serious and beyond a casual date. Which meant Chase intended to do his due diligence in vetting this guy for himself.

"So, how did the two of you meet?" he asked, jumping right into the interrogation.

Billie gave Chase an amused smile. "It's actually quite a funny story. Neil is the bachelor you replaced at the charity auction."

Chase's brows rose in surprise, but before he could respond, Billie continued on.

"Neil would have been Lauren's date to her sister's wedding, had he not been sick with the flu and I had to recruit you to take his place," she said, grinning. "Funny how fate works sometimes, huh?"

Another round of shock rippled through Chase. So, this was the guy that Lauren had been referring to when she'd charged into his office and said to him, *"You weren't my first choice of a bachelor, but I'm stuck with you."* She'd intended to bid on Neil, and knowing that, Chase couldn't help feeling a little territorial, which was ridiculous. It was definitely a twist he didn't see coming, and the thought that he might not have ever experienced being with Lauren made him realize what a gift his weekend with her had truly been.

Not wanting his thoughts to travel down that route again, he took a drink of his wine and refocused his attention on the happy couple across the table. "So, how did the two of you end up dating?"

Neil cleared his throat before answering the question. "Well, I felt incredibly bad about having to pull out of the auction at the last minute, so I showed up at the Future Fast Track offices with flowers to apologize, and a donation check. I took one look at Billie and I was quite taken with her so I didn't hesitate to ask her out for dinner."

Billie beamed affectionately at him before glancing back at Chase. "We discovered we had so much in common. We both love museums and Broadway shows, and while Neil might be an accountant, he loves the same video games that I do, like *Super Mario* and *Zelda*."

Neil grimaced, appearing a bit embarrassed. "You're making me look like a nerd in front of your brother."

"You are, just a little bit, which I absolutely adore about you." She leaned over and kissed his cheek, completely smitten with him. "You're this geeky, intellectual guy by day who crunches numbers, but once you leave the office, you are so much fun to hang out with."

Neil was smiling as he met Chase's gaze from across the table. "Honestly, it didn't take me long to realize that Billie is quite literally the dream girl I've been waiting for all my life."

Chase was truly happy for his sister, but the couple's infatuation with one another was almost too much for him to take. But even though their enthusiasm was over-the-top, he'd be lying if he didn't admit that he was envious of how the two of them made being together seem so easy and uncomplicated. Billie had far from a charmed upbringing, yet here she was, embracing the possibility of falling in love.

Their meals arrived, and while they ate, the conversation revolved around Billie telling Chase that she'd met Neil's parents and siblings over the past weekend, and how well it had gone. And how excited she was that she had an upcoming date with Neil's sister for the two of them to go to a place called Colorful Canvas, which was a wine and design class, whatever the hell that meant.

He listened to her go on, her genuine excitement making him smile. All during the course of dinner, he was both surprised and grateful that Billie didn't ask about his weekend with Lauren and figured she was too enamored with Neil so the question didn't cross her mind. Whatever the reason, Chase was relieved she kept up a steady stream of conversation that had nothing to do with him and his sad, wreck of a life.

After their main course, Billie ordered dessert, which she shared with Neil, while Chase opted for an Irish coffee.

When the pair finished the tiramisu, Neil stood up and smiled at Billie. "I know you want to talk to your brother privately, so I'm going to go and sit at the bar. You can come and get me when you're done."

"Thank you," she said, returning the smile with a soft one of her own.

Chase wasn't going to assume anything about what she wanted to have a private conversation with him about, and kept his tone casual as he asked, "Everything okay?"

She folded her arms on the table in front of her, her gaze direct and more serious than she'd been all evening. "With me, yes. As you can see, I'm great. I'm more concerned about you."

"Because?"

She pursed her lips together, the faintest amount of annoyance flickering in her eyes, which was something he didn't see often. "Oh, come on, Chase. Don't be obtuse."

He raised a brow and admitted to nothing.

"Okay, fine." She sighed heavily. "I called the Meridian today to discuss a few things with Lauren about next year's Future Fast Track charity ball. I know I've been in my own little bubble with Neil and should have called you earlier this week, but I didn't, so when I was on the phone with Lauren, I asked her how everything went this past weekend at her sister's wedding."

His gut twisted at just the mention of Lauren's name. "And?"

Billie held his gaze. "She said I should ask *you.*"

"It went just fine."

Her eyes narrowed on him. "Then why did Lauren sound so... sad? And not like her normal, upbeat self? Something happened between you two, didn't it?" she pressed. "And I'm not talking about sex, because... eww, you're my brother. But I can see it in your eyes, the same way I heard it in Lauren's voice. You've tried to be present tonight, and you've been great with Neil, but I know you, Chase. I've seen you when you're grumpy and annoyed and standoffish, but for the first time since meeting you, you look sad. Maybe even defeated."

He was so goddamn tired of trying to keep his walls raised high, of denying all the emotions that Lauren had cracked open inside him. "Yes," he finally admitted. "Something... happened. And it scared the goddamn shit out of me."

She broke out in a grin. "That's *good*."

He frowned at her in confusion. "Why is that good?"

"Because it tells me that your heart is working, and I don't mean in an obvious, pumping blood kind of way," she teased. "Being scared of feeling something means you're human, and I know it's hard to let yourself be vulnerable that way. And despite those walls you have up, and how gruff and tough you act, I already know you have the capacity to care very deeply."

He scoffed. "We've discussed my upbringing. What the hell do I really know about love, Billie?"

She looked taken aback. "You know how to love, Chase. If you didn't, I wouldn't be here, sitting across from you, feeling like the luckiest sister alive because you searched for me and found me and made me your family. A man incapable of love wouldn't have done that."

He sat back, not only listening to his sister, but processing her words. He'd been unhappy, not just for the last four days, but for most of his life. Until

Lauren.

"Chase, you can continue to bury yourself in work and tell yourself it's for the best or you can put that brain of yours to work and accept that things don't always have to be this way. *You* don't have to be this way. You don't have to be alone."

His hand curled around his empty espresso cup as he met Billie's gaze. "What if I hurt her?" he asked.

Billie leaned forward. "What do you think you're doing now?" she challenged him. "That said, I'm going back to Neil and leave you to your thoughts." She rose from her seat before he could push his chair back, and walked over and kissed his cheek. "Don't let this chance at happiness slip away, big brother."

She left him sitting there with the knowledge that he had one more chance to get this right with Lauren. Assuming she wasn't so upset with him she wanted nothing to do with him now. But knowing her sweet, forgiving personality, he didn't have much to worry about.

He just had to find the courage to approach her.

Chapter Sixteen

LAUREN MADE IT through the week on autopilot, barely aware of what she worked on, and by the time the weekend arrived, she was tired, weary, and wondering how long it was going to take for her to get over Chase. And if that was even possible.

After sleeping past noon on Saturday, which she never did, she finally shuffled out to the kitchen in her fuzzy slippers, not even caring that she looked a hot mess in her oldest, rattiest comfort pajamas, her hair an unkempt disarray around her head.

Her outward appearance definitely matched the morose way she was feeling inside, and she embraced the whole package, because it was her day off and she'd given herself this one last weekend to indulge in a good sulk before figuring out how she was going to explain to her parents and Gramps that she and Chase had called it quits. Her mother had left a few messages since the previous weekend, and Lauren called her back, only to get her voice mail. They'd been playing phone tag, but the truth of the matter was that she couldn't avoid the topic of Chase forever, so that excruciating conversation was on the weekend's docket. *Ugh.*

There was no denying that the painful way things had ended between them *had* felt as devastating as a breakup. Even more so than how things had ended with Greg, which told Lauren just how deeply she'd fallen for her grumpy, reluctant bachelor.

"Good morning!" Tara greeted her in a too chipper tone as her roommate exited her own bedroom, way too bright, fresh, and energetic for Lauren's mood. "Good of you to join the land of the living."

Lauren grunted in response as she rummaged through the refrigerator, grabbing the last container of the banana pudding she'd bought from a deli down the street. The rich, indulgent dessert with real bananas, whipped cream, and vanilla wafer cookies reminded her of the one her grandma used to make, and if this was her last day of wallowing, then she was going to make sure she at least enjoyed her favorite treat while she indulged in her pity party.

Taking her breakfast to the living room, she plopped down on the couch, removed the lid, and dove into the pudding.

Tara followed, eyeing her with genuine concern. "What is it going to take to snap you out of this funk you're in, because I gotta tell you, this is *not* a good look on you," she said, indicating Lauren's entire appearance with a wave of her hand.

"*This* is the look of having your heart crushed," she informed her friend.

Tara rolled her eyes, because yes, Lauren was being

dramatic and didn't care.

Tara crossed her colorfully tattooed arms over her chest. "Want me to go beat him up for you?"

Lauren cracked the first smile all week, even though Tara looked completely serious. "I appreciate the offer, but no. I'll be fine. I promise," she lied, because who really knew how long it took for a shattered heart to heal?

"I knew I should have set you up with one of the biker guys from the shop," she said, lips pursed. "Those types of bad boys are notorious heartbreakers, so at least you would have seen it coming."

Lauren ate the last bite of pudding, set the container on the table in front of the couch, then sighed. "Honestly? I have no regrets."

It was the truth. The memories she had with Chase were bittersweet, and she chose to focus on the sweeter aspects of their time together. Like the fun pictures of them in the photo booth, and those last few images where she and Chase were staring into each other's eyes, their connection and affection so evident.

Their pretend relationship might have started out as a ruse, but a man like Chase couldn't fake those kinds of emotions. She could see for herself how happy he'd been, but there was no forcing him to see the truth, or accept feelings he wasn't ready or willing to embrace.

A knock sounded on the door to their apartment, and Tara frowned. "Do not tell me you DoorDashed more junk food to eat."

Lauren shook her head. "No, I didn't. I have no idea who it is."

Tara walked to the door and opened it. "Oh," she exclaimed, causing Lauren to attempt to peer around her to see who was standing on the other side, but her roommate was blocking her view. "Those are beautiful," Tara said.

"They're for Lauren Connelly," a young man's voice said.

Lauren's heart skipped a beat. Who could be sending her flowers? And why?

"I'll take them." Tara gestured to Lauren behind her. "She's right over there and not really looking her best. I don't want to scare you off."

"Oh, my God," Lauren said in a disgruntled tone. "I don't look that bad!"

Tara turned around, holding a huge bouquet of flowers that were so big they covered her friend's face. "You kinda do," she said, peeking around the arrangement, as she headed toward the kitchen area. "Have you seen your hair?"

Lauren stood and smoothed a hand over the strands, grimacing as her fingers got caught in the tangles and snarls from not brushing it after waking up. *Whatever.*

"Well, well, well, I wonder who these are from," Tara drawled as she set the vase on the table, then removed the small envelope from the arrangement.

"That's mine, thank you very much." Reaching her

friend's side, Lauren plucked the note from Tara's fingers, her heart racing with a thousand hopeful probabilities, because only one person she could think of would send her flowers this elaborate. Blooms that undoubtedly cost a few hundred dollars, even if she didn't know *why* he'd sent them.

"Oh, she perks up," Tara teased.

Lauren rolled her eyes as she tore open the envelope then read the message inside, written in a masculine scrawl. *I'm not a pro at grand gestures, or even apologies, but you deserve them. Meet me for dinner tonight. Love, Chase.*

The breath left Lauren's lungs, and a giddy excitement permeated her entire body. The first part of that note made the heartache of the last week melt away, but it was the last two words, *Love, Chase*, that had the first glimmering signs of optimism blossoming inside her.

"Huh," Tara said from beside her. "Impressive. The guy certainly knows how to grovel, which is an important trait for any man to have. Are you going to meet him for dinner?"

"Of course I am," she said without any hesitation.

Her friend arched a pierced brow. "Even after everything he put you through?"

"I'm not going to lie. I hated everything about the way things ended between us last Sunday, but... I understand Chase enough to know that he needed this time and space to process how quick and intense things developed between us." She was just grateful that he came to what she hoped was a promising conclusion as the note indicated, instead of deciding Lauren was better off without him. Which she wasn't.

Another knock sounded at the door, and this time Lauren rushed over and made it there first, finding another delivery person, a woman, standing on the other side of the threshold holding a glossy black box with Oscar de la Renta stamped in gold on top, along with another envelope.

She thanked the woman, then brought the box over to the table and set it next to the vase of flowers. Tara's eyes nearly bugged out of her head when she saw the name of the designer on the box, while Lauren pulled the next message out of the envelope.

The note read, *I'm thinking positively and hope you've decided that your answer to meet me for dinner is a yes. Here's something for you to wear, but you would look beautiful in anything, or nothing at all. A driver will pick you up at 5:30. See you soon, Chase.*

Biting her bottom lip, Lauren lifted the lid and peeled back the tissue paper, gasping as she pulled out a cocktail dress in a gorgeous shade of dark pink. It was a simple silhouette with a sweeping neckline, a cinched waist, and a fluted skirt, but what made the dress so stunning was the small, crystal flower embellishments embroidered into the fabric. Clearly, Chase already knew her tastes. Also inside the box was a silver clutch and matching strappy heels.

"Holy shit," Tara breathed in awe. "He's pulling out all the stops. Your guy is not messing around, because a dress like that had to have set him back at least five grand, if not more."

Lauren winced at the amount, because she was certain Tara was right and damn, that was a lot of money. But she also realized how much time and effort all this planning had taken for this grand gesture and apology, all to make her feel special.

She spent the rest of the afternoon with Tara, feeling like Cinderella getting ready for the ball. After soaking in a fragrant bath, Tara helped her with her makeup and curling her hair, then zipping up the dress when it was almost time to go.

When the outfit was complete with the shoes and purse, Tara beamed at her, and Lauren smiled back, feeling like a princess, which wasn't something she'd ever thought of herself, at least not before Chase.

"Ahhh, now there's the Lauren I know and love," Tara said, grabbing her hand and giving it a squeeze. "The one with the vibrant sparkle in her eyes and the glow on her face, radiating happiness. Now go and get your man."

She planned to.

The driver arrived, and while the elaborate flowers and the over-the-top designer dress were wonderful, none of those things mattered to Lauren. The only thing that was important to her was Chase truly opening himself up to the possibility of falling in love with her. It was all she wanted, and she hoped that tonight was just the beginning for them.

She had no idea where she was going, but had another jaw-dropping moment as the car pulled up to the valet for Elysian Heights. An attendant opened her door and helped her out, and she walked into the exclusive restaurant, which was surprisingly... not busy and fairly quiet for a Saturday evening, except for the faint sound of classical music playing in the background.

Frowning in confusion, she stepped up to the woman standing behind the hostess stand, who smiled at her.

"I assume you're here for Chase Gossard?" she asked, as if nothing was out of the ordinary.

Lauren nodded. "Yes, I am."

"He's waiting for you in the dining area. Right this way."

She followed the woman to a set of double mahogany doors, which she opened, revealing a room with just one table in the middle, and Chase standing beside it in a tailored suit, the entire restaurant empty of any other guests.

She gaped in shock, wondering how in the world Chase had managed such a feat, and how he'd known about her secret desire to eat at Elysian Heights.

"Enjoy your evening, Ms. Connelly," the woman said pleasantly, then closed the doors behind her as she retreated, leaving Lauren alone with Chase.

CHASE COULDN'T RECALL ever being so nervous as he

watched Lauren slowly approach him, her eyes wide as she took in the interior of the quiet restaurant, her gaze slowly landing on him. He walked toward her, too, meeting her halfway.

She smiled, and that was all he needed to see to know that everything was going to be okay. She looked so radiant in the pink dress that conformed to her curves, her eyes sparkling with awe and a flush on her beautiful face. She was such a breath of fresh air when he'd been suffocating for far too long, and she made him want to be a better man, just for her.

And dear God, he just wanted to drop to his knees in front of her and beg her to forgive him for being such a dumbass the previous weekend. But he already knew there was no need for that. This woman knew all the parts of him, the good, the bad, and the ugly, and she'd already accepted him, flaws and all. It had just taken him a little longer to figure his shit out.

Last weekend, he'd honestly believed he was being noble, that in letting her go, he was protecting her from the emotionally damaged man he believed himself to be. His talk with Billie had been a defining moment, where he'd realized that ending things with Lauren had been all about his own self-preservation, wrapped up in false heroism. He hadn't been saving her from him. All he'd been doing was denying himself the chance to know and experience the kind of love she gave so freely, no strings attached.

Reaching her, he took Lauren's hand and tucked it into the crook of his arm as he escorted her back to the table. He held out Lauren's chair and waited until she was seated before joining her in the seat across from her.

She looked around in confusion, taking in the elegant décor before her gaze came back to his. "I, uh, don't understand."

He tipped his head and smiled at her. "What are you having a hard time comprehending?"

"This is quite the grand gesture," she teased him, easing any last lingering traces of anxiety he might have been feeling. "But... I mean... *how?*"

"How did I know you wanted to dine at Elysian Heights?" he asked, trying to guess what she was asking. "Your gramps mentioned it."

She shook her head, causing the soft waves in her hair to brush along her shoulders. "No, I mean, it's a Saturday night and we're the only ones here, at a restaurant that books out *months* in advance."

Oh, yeah, *that.* He smirked and shrugged. "I might have pulled a few strings to make it happen. The owner is a client." Not to mention, he'd paid a pretty penny to have the existing reservations rescheduled, and the dining room all to themselves for the next two hours.

"And the dress..." she said softly. "You shouldn't have."

"I'm glad I did," he replied without hesitation. "You look... breathtaking."

A pink blush swept across her cheeks. "All this... it's too much."

He disagreed. "You're worth every fucking penny, sweetheart. I realized that spoiling you makes me happy, so you might as well get used to it."

Before she could respond, they were interrupted by the only waiter in the dining area as he came to their table with the bottle of wine Chase had ordered earlier, and poured them each a glass. Oliver introduced himself, then gave them an overview of what to expect for their five-course tasting menu, which was being prepared by celebrity chef Rand Turro, himself.

The meal started immediately, and wanting Lauren to enjoy the complete Elysian Heights experience, he deliberately kept their conversation light. The last thing he wanted to do was to ruin the atmosphere with a serious discussion, though he knew it was going to happen before the night was over. There were things he wanted to say to her, things she needed to hear.

Instead, he watched Lauren's delightful reaction to everything. How she *oohed* and *awwed* over the presentation of each course, and the way she moaned and made the sexiest noises as she savored each and every bite of food.

Chef Rand came to their table at one point, and Chase had to swallow back his laughter at how cute Lauren was with the other man, gushing over his food and blushing and stammering on about how she loved watching him on the reality competition show.

After finishing her little trio of desserts, she sat back in her chair with a happy, contented sigh. "That was amazing."

"I'm glad you enjoyed it."

She placed her linen napkin down and held his gaze from across the table. "So, what prompted all this?"

"If I'm being honest, Billie," he said, rubbing his palm along his jaw. "After a miserable week at work, I met her for dinner on Thursday. She introduced me to her new boyfriend, Neil Pierson, the guy I took the place of at the bachelor auction."

Lauren grinned. "She mentioned that they were dating, and she seems very smitten with him."

"They're quite well matched," he agreed. "More so than you and he would have been. I should have thanked him for getting sick and pulling out of the auction."

Her eyes widened, hope shimmering in the depths. "Why?"

"Because if he hadn't, I never would have met you," he said, the words coming far easier than he ever would have imagined, because they were real, true, and heartfelt. "I would have missed out on the best thing that has happened in my life, besides finding Billie. I would have never known what it was like to be in the presence of a woman who makes me smile and laugh more than I ever had. You've challenged me, you've made me take a good, hard look at my past, and I'm so ready to let go of all the bitterness and resentment that has been weighing me down for too long."

She stood up and came around the table to his side, then sat on his lap, looping her arms around his neck. "You're doing so well," she said with one of the playful grins that he loved. "Tell me more."

He laughed gruffly, his hands settling on the curves of her waist as he met, and held, her gaze. "We both already know what an idiot I was to let you walk away last weekend."

She bit her bottom lip, her eyes flashing with humor. "I'm not going to argue with that."

He dug even deeper, to make sure she understood how much of an impact she'd had on him. "What you made me feel in a very short time... I've never been through so many emotions. I've never felt that kind of longing and need that I did for you, and I'd be lying if I didn't say that scared the shit out of me."

"It's okay to be afraid," she said softly, her fingers caressing the nape of his neck. "Entrusting another person with your heart is a scary and vulnerable thing, and so is falling in love. But it's so worth the risk."

"*You* are worth the risk," he said, needing her to know that he was ready and willing to take that leap of faith with her. "Do you remember what you said to me after I told you about my past, at the park? That there are crossroads that we come to in our lives and we can choose to stay on the same beaten path, wishing things were different, or we can make an altogether better choice and alter the direction of our future?"

She nodded. "Yes."

"Well, I choose *you*, Lauren Connelly. You're the path I want to follow into the future." He reached up a hand and gently cupped her cheek, and she didn't hesitate to nuzzle into his palm. "Just be patient with me," he said. "This is all new to me, and I have no doubt I'm going to fuck up now and then."

She laughed huskily. "No relationship is perfect, but you're perfect for me."

He slid his hand into her hair and pressed his forehead to hers. "How is that even possible?"

She grinned at him and pressed her body closer to his. "You just have a grumpy charm about you that I can't resist."

She shifted on his lap and he groaned, suddenly all too aware of just how well her ass was positioned against his cock. "I'm ready to move on to the next part of the evening, how about you?"

She did that slight shimmy thing again with her hips, deliberately tempting him this time. "Which part would that be?"

He placed his lips near her ear. "Taking you home and disheveling the fuck out of you."

She shivered at those familiar words, and when she pulled her head back, the need in her eyes matched the one in his soul. "Yes, I would like that very much, please."

He chuckled, and couldn't get Lauren out of there and alone fast enough.

As he drove them toward his place, feeling happier than ever, he knew one thing for certain. All the things that had once tethered him to the past no longer mattered. Only the future did, with Lauren by his side.

Forever.

Epilogue

WHAT A DIFFERENCE a year made.

Lauren glanced around the crowded Meridian ballroom, elaborately decorated for the annual Future Fast Track charity event, finally able to relax now that dinner had been served and the guests were mingling before the bachelor auction started.

She glanced across the room near the bar, where a group of men were gathered—Chase conversing with Derek Bettencourt, Drew and Tripp Daniels, and Neil, who was now engaged to Billie. Some of the same men who'd been auctioned off the previous year but were now off the market and in exclusive relationships as a result of those pairings. Who knew the Future Fast Track bachelor auction would produce more committed couples than the actual bachelor franchise?

"You've outdone yourself once again," Billie said, coming up beside Lauren.

"Thank you." Lauren smiled at her friend and soon-to-be sister-in-law, who was wearing a gorgeous strapless gown in sapphire blue, which matched the streak of color in her blonde hair.

Over the past year, Lauren's boss, Jade Dare, had

passed on even more responsibilities to her so she could spend more time at home with her baby daughter, Sage. And recently, Skye, her assistant—who was married to Tripp—had taken time off for maternity leave, which had increased Lauren's workload, but she thrived on the challenge and the pressure of putting together an event. Especially when it all came together so seamlessly.

"I'm betting Neil is relieved that he's not up on the auction block this year," Lauren teased Billie.

"Not a chance," she said with a laugh, and raised her left hand, showing off the engagement ring the other man had recently put on her finger. "He's all mine."

Lauren understood the sentiment, because she felt the same way about Chase. After that evening at Elysian Heights, there hadn't been a day when they'd gone without talking or seeing one another. Six months ago, she'd moved in with Chase, and two months after that he'd asked her to marry him. She'd very enthusiastically answered with *yes* as he'd slipped an obscenely large diamond ring on her finger.

Lauren started as she felt arms slip around her waist from behind and a strong, male body press tight against her as he pulled her close. Recognizing the scent of Chase's cologne, she immediately relaxed in his embrace.

"Sorry to interrupt, but I'm going to steal away my fiancée before the bachelor auction starts," he said to Billie from over Lauren's shoulder.

Billie smiled at her brother, the fondness for him unmistakable in her eyes. "Okay, but you two behave yourself."

"I make no promises," he said, the playfulness in his voice now a more normal occurrence than his previously gruff tone of a year ago.

Lauren grinned, her heart swelling with affection and love. Her man had come a long way since she'd first met him as a grumpy, cantankerous bachelor who'd built a fortress around his heart and viewed the world through a lens of skepticism. He was a different man now. A better man. One who enjoyed life and no longer carried the burden of his past.

He had transformed in ways she could hardly have imagined a year ago. His once furrowed brow had softened, replaced by genuine smiles and laughter that lit up his handsome face. It had taken time and patience on Lauren's part, but the walls he'd erected had eventually crumbled to dust, and in their place was a warmth and openness that only made her fall more in love with him.

Grabbing Lauren's hand, he led her out of the ballroom to an alcove with a balcony that was vacant.

"What's all this about?" she asked, turning to face him when they were standing side by side at the railing, overlooking Manhattan.

He shrugged and gently brushed a strand of hair away from her cheek. "Just thought you could use a breath of fresh air. I've watched you run around for the past few hours, and I realized that I miss you when you're not by my side."

"Aww, look at you," she said, looping her arms around his neck, loving how openly affectionate he was with her these days. "You're so romantic."

He rolled his eyes at that and placed his hands at the small of her back. "I just wanted to check to make sure you're doing okay."

"I'm doing great," she replied, sighing contentedly. "Especially right now, in this moment with you." Because *he* was all she needed.

"I have to agree," he murmured, and pressed his lips to hers in a soft, sweet kiss before lifting his head again. "I love you, Lauren soon-to-be Gossard, and I can't wait to marry the fuck out of you."

She laughed, since that phrase had become somewhat of an inside joke between the two of them. "I can't wait, either," she said, knowing that a lifetime of happiness and endless, exciting possibilities awaited them.

Thanks for reading! Up next is **JUST A LITTLE CRUSH**, a story in Carly Phillips' Sterling family world, featuring Caleb Kane and Stevie Griffen from **JUST ONE MORE MOMENT** (Remy and Raven's story). Caleb is Raven's brother, and we're so excited to bring you his story with Stevie, who works at The Back Door Bar.

Other books in the Dare Crossover Bachelor Auction Series:

For Book News:
SIGN UP for Carly's Newsletter:
carlyphillips.com/CPNewsletter
SIGN UP for Erika's Newsletter:
geni.us/ErikaWildeNewsletter

Carly Phillips and Erika Wilde Booklist

A Dare Crossover Series
Just A Little Hookup
Just A Little Secret
Just A Little Promise
Just A Little Chase
Just A Little Crush

Dirty Sexy Series
Dirty Sexy Saint
Dirty Sexy Inked
Dirty Sexy Cuffed
Dirty Sexy Sinner

Book Boyfriend Series
Big Shot
Faking It
Well Built
Rock Solid

The Boyfriend Experience

About the Authors

CARLY PHILLIPS is the bestselling author of over eighty sexy contemporary romances featuring hot men, strong women, and the emotionally compelling stories her readers have come to expect and love. She is happily married to her college sweetheart and the mother of two adult daughters and their crazy dogs. She loves social media and is always around to interact with her readers. You can find out more and get two free books at www.carlyphillips.com.

ERIKA WILDE is the author of the sexy Marriage Diaries series and The Players Club series. She lives in Oregon with her husband and two daughters, and when she's not writing you can find her exploring the beautiful Pacific Northwest. For more information on her upcoming releases, please visit website at www.erikawilde.com.

Made in the USA
Monee, IL
16 September 2024

65956152R10128